POCHO

POCHO

JOSÉ ANTONIO VILLARREAL

ANCHOR BOOKS
A DIVISION OF RANDOM HOUSE, INC.
NEW YORK

Dedico este libro a mi padre, José Heladio Villarreal, y, a la memoria de mi madre, Felícitaz R. Villarreal.

ANCHOR BOOKS EDITIONS, 1970, 1989

Copyright © 1959 by José Antonio Villarreal

All rights reserved under International and Pan-American Copyright Conventions. Published in the United States by Anchor Books, a division of Random House, Inc., New York, and simultaneously in Canada by Random House of Canada Limited, Toronto. Originally published in hardcover in the United States by Doubleday in 1959. The Anchor Books edition is published by arrangement with Doubleday, a division of Random House, Inc.

Anchor Books and colophon are registered trademarks of Random House, Inc.

Library of Congress Cataloging-in-Publication Data
Villarreal, José Antonio.
    Pocho / José Antonio Villarreal.
    —Anchor Books ed.
        p. cm.
    I. Title
PS3572.I37P6 1989   89-18204
813'.54—dc20   CIP
ISBN 0-385-06118-8

www.anchorbooks.com

PRINTED IN THE UNITED STATES OF AMERICA

40 39 38 37 36 35 34 33 32

ONE

A light snow was falling as the train from Mexico City pulled into Ciudad Juárez. A film of ice had formed on the wooden sidewalks, and the unpaved streets were deep in mud where the wagons and automobiles had sludged through. A man got off the train and elbowed his way through the crowd that inevitably gathered at the arrival of a train from the capital. Ten years earlier, as a young man of eighteen, he had come to this same city in not so quiet a fashion. Then he had been a cavalry officer in Villa's army that took Juárez, northern lifeline to the United States, from the forces of the government. A few months later, he had returned with the great General to retake the city after it had been sold out to the enemy by the army Villa had left there to protect it.

As he walked along the crowded streets, he almost wished for the old days, and carelessly wondered how many men he had killed here. His leather pants legs showed he wore the traditional tight-fitting costume of the Mexican charro. The other two-thirds of his body was encased in a huge mackinaw. On his head was a large, heavy hat, the string of which hung loosely behind, reaching down the nape of his neck. His once fair skin had been turned a ruddy color by years of outdoor life and now gave his blue-gray eyes an odd, cold mien. Although he was not an inordinately large man, the mackinaw and the sombrero made him dwarf the people around him. He walked aimlessly along the streets, carried on and directed by the crowd, until finally he turned into a cantina. He chose a

1

corner table and hung his heavy coat on a nail behind him. He arranged himself on the chair so his gun hung loose and his arm had freedom of movement.

It was still early in the day, but the cantina was full and lively. A mariachi was playing sentimental ballads of unrequited love, and on a table across the large room a young girl was dancing a jarabe tapatío to the olés of a group of men, an occasional glint of brown thigh visible as she nimbly moved her small feet around the brim of the sombrero.

A waiter approached the stranger, and he ordered the meal of the day and a bottle of mezcal. He sat there eating and drinking, seemingly oblivious to the din and gaiety about him. One or two women attempted to sit at his table, but with a shake of his head he sent them away. When he was through eating, he washed his mouth with a half tumbler of liquor and spat on the floor. The girl who had been dancing on the table went by him and disappeared in the enclosure to his left. He heard the hard, steady hiss as she relieved herself on the earthen floor. As she walked past him, he called, "Come here!"

She hesitated in mid-stride. The words, although spoken in a low voice, had been commanding. "¿Qué quieres?" She spoke in the familiar. In a cantina, as in bed, courtesy was nonexistent. Outside was another thing.

"I have been watching you. You please me."

"So? I please many men," she said, very sure of herself, and made as if to leave.

"Sit down and drink with me," he said.

She knew she should go, but something about him frightened her and she lost her composure. "Even if I wanted to do so, I could not." She did not realize she was explaining to this man, a complete stranger. "My friends are waiting for me."

"Your friends? Oh, *those?*" he pointed and laughed. "No, little one, you are a woman and deserve better. Sit here."

She sat down nervously at the edge of the seat. She kept her head lowered as she spoke. "My lover is over there. He does not mind if I work when he is not here, but he is

2

here now and I must entertain his friends." She looked up at him, sure of herself once more. She patted his hand and said very professionally, "Be good and come back tomorrow. Then I will be good to you. I am told I am very good."

"No. You are with me now. I have not had a woman in a week, and am better for you than your pimp."

The blood that came to her face erased her smile. She started to rise. He reached for her arm and easily pulled her back into the chair. He pushed his glass to her.

"I cannot drink this," she said. "It is too strong." She rubbed the four white spots on her arm where his fingers had momentarily stopped the circulation. She wondered how after six months of this life she could still blush.

He said, "Some milk, perhaps."

"He is coming now. *Please!* He is a bad one!" One of the men had detached himself from the group across the room. His friends watched with half interest. He would return with his woman.

He walked to the girl and spoke in a cultured voice. "Come, you have kept us waiting." She did not answer. It was out of her hands now.

"This one stays with me," said the stranger.

The other ignored him. "Can you not hear, deaf one? Get up!" he said to the girl.

"Do not worry, señor." The voice of the man at the table was very matter-of-fact. "I have money and you will get your share."

"Gentlemen do not speak of such things, señor. You are being insulting."

"Ah, then a gentleman procurer must never mention the fact, is that it?" His voice was still soft, almost friendly, despite the mockery of the words.

The girl's lover made an effort to control his voice. "Come," he said to her. "You are not in the country now. You need not associate with peones."

"The peón has larger balls than the city-bred gachupín," said the charro. "Now go back to your friends. We are tired of you."

"Son of the great mother whore!" the other screamed.

3

"I gave you your chance to live!" His gun was barely out of its shoulder holster when the bullet hit him above the groin. The stranger calmly shot him once more as he lay writhing on the floor; his gun had been in his hand all along. He took his coat and, without a look at the crowd, pulled the girl out of the cantina.

In the hotel he said, "You can stop crying now and take off my boots." When they were in bed, he asked, "How old are you?"

"I have fifteen years." After a moment she said, "You have not asked me my name."

"¿Qué importa?" he said.

The man was awakened a few hours later by the clatter of feet outside the door. He had his hand on his gun as the room was suddenly filled by uniformed men.

"Please do not resist, señor. You are under arrest," said a young lieutenant, who was in command. "You will dress, please, and accompany me."

"May I take my woman?"

"Why not?" The lieutenant shrugged his shoulders. He unabashedly kept his eyes on the girl as they dressed. "May I compliment your taste, señor?"

"Thank you," said the prisoner. "But you surprise me. By the manner in which you came in, I did not think you had the sense of love."

"I am not an ox. I feel deeply the intrusion, but, you know, the other died."

"But of course. It could be no other way." He was dressed now. "Do we walk or ride, Teniente?"

"We walk. It is not far."

They arrived at a stockade that covered a complete city square. A large building for administrative purposes stood in one corner. The remainder of the stockade held no buildings other than the flimsy, wooden lean-tos the prisoners used to protect them from the elements. Here and there, the prisoners' children were seen huddled together to keep warm, while their mothers cooked over their small open fires. The man and woman were taken

4

into a room where the lieutenant seated himself behind a small desk.

"Please be seated. The mere formality of a form or two for the Commandant. It is for him to decide when you are to be shot." The young lieutenant was very business-like.

"First, a favor, if you please."

"Yes?"

"Have a man escort the woman back to the hotel. I did not know what a pigsty you have here," said the man.

"Immediately," said the lieutenant. "We do the best we can here, señor. We will have better accommodations before long." He was still polite, but the stranger was beginning to irritate him, so he added, "By then, of course, you will not be concerned about the matter."

"You are kind, Lieutenant. Where did you make your rank?"

"At the National Academy, naturally." He became impatient and a little angry. "Come, señor. This is not exactly a social call. I will ask the questions, please. Your name?"

"Juan Rubio."

"How long have you been in Juárez?"

"I arrived today from México."

"It is obvious that you are not from the capital. Of what nature was your business there?"

"I do not see how that concerns this matter, but since you ask, I was attending the National Military Academy."

The young lieutenant smiled in disbelief. "Come, now, señor," he said complacently. "You surely do not expect me to believe that. A man of your station?" Juan Rubio said nothing, and suddenly the lieutenant said excitedly, "Wait! You cannot possibly be Juan Manuel Rubio? The Colonel Rubio?"

"The ex-Colonel Rubio, but at your service nevertheless, Teniente. You know of me?"

"Rubio of Santa Rosalía, Torreón, Zacatecas, and even here, Juárez. No one speaks more highly of you than the General. . . . But what have I done? Ah! You do not know the position in which you have put me by being who

5

you are." He paced the narrow room nervously. "I must call the General at once. He will degrade me to the ranks, no matter that I was but following his own orders. . . . He thinks of you as his son, you know." He picked up the telephone and rang hurriedly. "¡Bueno! I wish to speak to the General, please. . . . Teniente Ramos here. . . . Yes, yes, I know, but this is highly important to the General himself. . . . No, I must speak to him personally. . . . A matter of importance, I say. . . . Yes, I assume the responsibility." He pounded his fist lightly on the table as he waited for his connection. "¡Bueno! Teniente Ramos speaking. . . . A matter of high importance, mi general. . . . I have the prisoner whose arrest you ordered. . . . ¡No, no mi general! His name is Juan Manuel Rubio. . . . Yes. . . . Yes, your prerogative entirely, mi general. . . . Yes, sir. Thank you, sir." He slowly put the receiver down. "He said he will personally flog me for bringing you here," he said to Juan. "He will be here immediately."

Juan laughed. "Do not worry," he said. "If it is who I think it is, nothing will happen to you because of this."

"Fuentes." The young lieutenant was sad.

"Old Hermilio. I thought as much. Ah, the noise he can make, but that is all."

"Yes, but these old dogs of the Revolution—one can never tell what they will do next." He reddened suddenly. "My apologies, mi coronel. I forgot that you, too, came of the Revolution."

"Forget it," said Juan. "It was not an insult."

There was a noise in the hallway, and the General, accompanied by two officers, walked into the small room. He was short and fat, and his mustache was white. He went directly to Juan and put his arms around him. They exchanged the abrazo, the informal embrace between two close friends.

"Ah, Juan Manuel! What pleasure! It is good to see you."

"¡Quihúbole, Hermilio, quihúbole!" They spoke to each other in the provincial accent, the dialect of the peón.

"Fine, fine, but let us go, Juan Manuel. My car is out-

6

side," the General said. "And you, cabrón, I will take care of you later," he said to the lieutenant.

A few minutes later, they were at the General's home. The General handed him a glass of aguardiente and said:

"That was a wrong thing you did today, Juan Manuel."

"He was a Spaniard," Juan said.

"But surely you are not too stupid to realize that you cannot personally rid this world of the Spaniard!"

"I am not concerned with the world, mi general. But someday they must be driven out of México."

"My sentiments exactly, but this one, Juan Manuel—this one was a very rich one."

"Are not all of them?"

"Yes, but this one was from the other side. You know what that means now that we are friendly with the gringos."

"Ah, Hermilio! Of what good was all the fighting? The Spanish milk still flows into our women!"

"I know. We are no better off than we were before, but the problem now is how to get you away from here. Juárez has changed, and one cannot get away with such things around here now. Our proximity to the norteamericanos makes it imperative that we have an orderly city. We are so near to the other side that one errant bullet could do irreparable harm to our relationship."

"Yes, we *are* close to the other side," said Juan. "Remember the times we took this place, how we could not effectively employ our artillery because a slight miscalculation would have sent shells into El Paso del Norte? And remember how the gringos were all on the other side of the Bravo watching the fighting. We were like toreros those times—we had our aficionados."

"It seems like only yesterday, Juan Manuel," said the General wistfully. "But, to return to the problem at hand, the order for your arrest came from the capital. Telegraphed in less than four hours from the time of the incident. So, you see, the deceased had influence. All this trouble because you got yourself hot for a whore!"

"You did not see her, Hermilio. Even you, old as you are, would want her."

"I am still able, you crazy," said the General. "Why

did you not come to me if you wanted a woman? You should see the ones that come here. Beautiful and well-bred—even gringas, if you have a taste for them."

"*Well-bred,*" Juan mimicked. "You talk like a great don, old one. Did you forget the big white breeches and the huaraches when you received this command? Do you not remember that our people have better manners than this aristocracy, that our ancestors were princes in a civilization that was possibly more advanced than this one? I had enough of your high-class women in México. And as for the pale ones, they do not please me, either. No, my general with good manners, the india is still the most beautiful woman in the world."

"Forgive me, Juan Manuel," said the General. "Your rebuke was well deserved. Living in this society makes me talk like the people in it. I have not really forgotten my heritage. We are provincials, you and I, first and last. Tell me, why did you leave México?"

"I got tired of playing soldier with idiots. When that one-armed bastard Obregón offered to send the old officers to the Academy, I did not think it would be as it was. Believe me, my general, there we were, Grijalva, Orozco, López—the cross-eyed one—and other such men. You know them all, every one of them a valiant soldier. I myself campaigned almost ten years with don Pancho! And a snotty cadet sergeant with the walk of a maricón would come up and say, 'Straighten up! Button up your blouse! Clean your boots!' Then, every day for two hours in the morning and two hours before dinner, it was walk, walk, walk—and me a cavalry officer—and the little fag would say, 'To the right! To the left! Attention! You are now in the National Army of México—try to look like soldiers!' Can you imagine a simple shit like that, my general? After ten years, this capón tells me to look like a soldier!

"And the classes, Hermilio. You cannot imagine the number of books we had to read, books on strategy written by the same generals we defeated. The instructors were all from the old government army. Some of them I recognized from the rear, having seen them a number of times running barefaced from battle. They were teaching

8

us tactics, and here I was practically reared by the greatest tactician of them all! We asked them to drill us on horses, and were told that was only for third-year men. I could not wait three years for a horse, so one afternoon, when the men were out drilling, I sneaked off to the stables and borrowed a horse and a reata. I did not have time to steal a saddle, so I tied the end of the rope to my waist. I rode out on the drill field, screaming and shouting, and the men broke ranks and ran. I roped the cadet sergeant by one leg and dragged him around until he stopped screaming. Ah, what diversion, my general. The young students were frightened, certain that I had gone mad, but the old soldiers stood in one group, laughing in guffaws, and they gave me a *viva* as I left. No one tried to stop me.

"I returned that night with some tequila, and we had a fiesta in the barracks. We tied the new cadet sergeant up, until we got him drunk and he would not dare call the guard. Some of us sneaked out and smuggled some women in, and that crazy Grijalva brought back a full mariachi. Seven musicians he brought in at the point of a gun! He said he had taken the gun away from a gendarme. Ay, that crazy! The youngsters in the barracks joined in the fun, and when the guard came up, they strapped him to a bunk. Ah, what a delicious time we had, my general, until finally a platoon of armed men was sent to investigate, and I had a devil of a time getting away." Both men were laughing by the time Juan finished the narrative.

"Ah, what I would give for your youth, Juan Manuel," said the General. "And the cadet sergeant?"

"A broken arm and leg, that was all."

"Then what did you do?"

"The next day I went to see General Paz. I told him I wished to retire from the army, but he persuaded me to take a leave of absence until I decided what I wanted to do. He is a fine man and a brave one, but he is on the way out." His voice grew serious. "The purge is on, my general. Villa has removed himself from active duty, but Obregón knows he must get rid of certain others before he can feel safe."

9

"Yes," said the General, "I know. I have already applied for my retirement, and soon will be returning to my pueblo. I think I will be left alone and in peace there. Obregón does not trust Villistas, but he fears only the General now that Felipe Angeles is dead. Every day, I wait word of the Chief's assassination."

"Don Pancho can still take care of himself."

"Not now. You know how he is living. Openly, not in the mountains. And he has but a few men with him. No," he said sadly, "I am resigned that his death is inevitable."

"But what irony," said Juan bitterly. "Villa, a man like ourselves and almost illiterate, was driven to brilliant victories by his noble illusion. With Obregón, a delusion was the driving force. Now the great one waits almost passively for an assassin's bullet while the nation he won is in the hands of the bastard opportunist."

"The destiny," said the General. "Who can go contrary to the destiny?"

Juan did not attempt to answer. He was suddenly filled with such hopelessness that he was inarticulate. His beloved general was to die—perhaps already he was dead! And all the dead in the struggle had died for nothing, and the living who had followed him would live also for nothing. But, no! He could not allow himself to believe such a thing! Such a monstrous thing should not be even thought by him! He spoke aloud with conviction. "They will not kill him. They cannot! By God! You know the man—you have seen the things he does, the risks he takes. I picture him now, calmly sitting his horse, watching the battle with his cold eyes, while twenty thousand Mausers were shooting at his figure and all around him men were falling. It was die, die, die, that day—truly it was a day for dying. And I came near him, purely by accident, for I belonged on the opposite flank, but by now there was no opposite flank, and he said, 'Juan Manuelito'—he will say things like that sometimes—'they are killing me too many people. It would be better if they would go over where the enemy is to die than here.' You would have thought that we were alone in that meadow, the way he talked. 'I need an example, muchacho. Go over and bring me that field-piece that is irritating me so much.' He was telling me to go die for him and it might help him win his battle and I knew it, but at that moment if he had asked me to turn my backside and submit to him, I would have done it without a qualm. So I rode toward the enemy, with reata in hand, but before I reached the little cannon, my horse was killed. But that was enough. Our men advanced, and the battle was won. How can they kill a man like that—a man with such balls! He walks with God, although the curates would deny it. If he wills it so, he can live forever!"

The General's voice was compassionate, and both men were unashamed of their tears. "Perhaps that is the answer, Juan Manuel," he said. "Perhaps the hour of his death is near because he wills it so."

"I will not believe it," said Juan. "It *cannot* be so." They were silent for a moment, and then Juan spoke; he addressed the old man not only as a friend but as the mature man he was. "Although I told them at the capital that I would take a year's leave of absence, within myself I have retired from the army. It is impossible for me to be a soldier for Obregón. The few weeks that I was gave me a feeling that I was not clean. I truly felt that I could better help my people if I went to the Academy, but I know differently now. I could be a general within five years, but I would have to become like the rest of them in power —be, in fact, one of them. Then I would spend so much time exploiting my people that I would have no time to help them.

"I came here because this is where the General will strike first when he returns. It is the only way to help México now. He will come back, and the people will follow him once again, and he will liberate the nation for the third time. And I wait here until he sends for me."

The old General shook his head sadly. "It is a great thing, this belief that you still have, Juan Manuel, but it is a bad thing, too, because it is futile. There has been too much war—too much blood. So much that to spill more would destroy the country completely. Yet, knowing this, I wish I could feel like you. But I am tired also of this

11

bloodletting, and the people are sick of it. And now the biggest factor is that Obregón is recognized by the United States. Also, he is stronger, and no matter how you feel about the man, he is a soldier—indeed, you cannot deny he is a soldier."

"I would be stupid to deny that after Celaya," said Juan, but he refused to be discouraged. "Nevertheless, I know my General Villa," he said. "And I will wait as long as he sees fit. If he sends for me tonight, I am prepared to go."

"I grieve for you, my son. But you know you cannot remain here after that of this morning."

"What do you propose to do with me?" asked Juan. He had completely forgotten that a few hours ago he had killed a man.

"You can return to Zacatecas if you wish."

"I have many enemies there. There would be killing after killing, until one day I would have an unlucky day."

"Consuelo and the children, are they there?"

"I left her in Torreón with her people when I went to México."

"You have deserted her?" asked the General.

"I do not know yet," answered Juan.

The General was about to say something, then changed his mind. A man's family was his personal matter. He thought for a minute. "I think the safest place for you at present is across the bridge. Have you ever been to the other side?"

"Only to Columbus," answered Juan.

The General looked surprised and pleased. He looked at Juan with pride and respect, and there was a quality almost of possessiveness in his attitude as he spoke. "You have never told me that before. There are not many of you left."

"You have never asked me before."

"There is something going on across the border that I have not told you," said the General. "Because it is a great futility and, too, because you would not be satisfied with that kind of action, or inaction, I do not wish that you become involved in it. The thing is, there are men in

El Paso who are even now working to raise the funds necessary to start another offensive. When they are done with their plotting and their propaganda, they plan to contact Villa. He, meanwhile, is in Canutillo, and does not even know this is going on."

"I know the breed," said Juan. "Exiled politicians seeking a soft billet. I have seen them through the years. Mysterious little people hiding in jacales, always talking, always plotting—I do not trust them."

The General laughed at him. "You are too hotheaded, Juan Manuel. I should not have worried about your becoming mixed up in their intrigues. Your anger is reassuring. And yet there is a place for the politicians in all this. They have their place. And the plotters and thinkers with the business suits—they have their place also. Madero was the greatest thinker and plotter of them all. He was the one responsible for all this. Perhaps he was the one to blame."

Juan Rubio understood, and yet he was angry. "But he was for the Mexican—for the people. You may blame him for the suffering and for the killing, but that was a necessity, and the nation has been liberated and will again be liberated. Obregón is not immortal, you know." He stopped for a moment as an idea crossed his mind. He shook his head and continued, "The thing about little men in business suits that disturbs me is that somewhere, at this very moment perhaps, there is such a group of these animals mapping out the manner in which my general can be caught unawares. Obregón is a soldier, and a good one, but this type of thing must be done for him by civilians. And, being the kind of people they are, they will undoubtedly corrupt someone near Villa with money and promises, or both, to betray him."

"Ah," sighed the General. "It is true—so true! But, tell me, did you for a minute there think of killing the President?"

Now Juan Manuel could laugh once more. "You are a sly old one," he said. "Many times I have wished that he should die. I have never until just a moment ago had the urge to do myself that favor."

13

"You will not be foolish . . ."

"I love life, even though you might think I do not. I could do that only if it meant that immediately everything would change. The death of Obregón is not the answer, for there are men like him, even though they are not strong in the military way, who would take his place, because now no one is opposing them. I could not die for that. And yet if my general Villa should ask that of me . . ."

The General stood up suddenly, and Juan knew he had made a decision. "Come, I will get you a change of clothing. Tonight I must secret you across the border. I have the bite on a gringo cattleman, and will give you a letter for him."

"What kind of bite?"

"Oh, I simply do not notice that he smuggles cattle across the Bravo."

"Goddamn it!" said Juan. "You too? Are there no honest people left? Is honor that worthless?"

"My hands are tied, Juan Manuel," said the General. "One might say the bribe goes with the command here. Almost a matter of courtesy on the part of the gringos. Anyway, you should be pleased, for the cattle is being stolen from the Spaniards."

"That is a point for it, but still it is very little justification for your actions. I wonder that you are helping me, for it seems that we are on opposite sides now. You have grown fat, old one."

"I have grown old, my son," said the General sadly. "You do me an injustice, and I can only grieve."

Juan looked at the old soldier, and he could not keep his contempt from showing. "Where is that courage—where has it gone? There is nothing left for you, old one. There is no need for you to retire, for you have retired already. Stay here. There is no danger that *you* might be marked for death. Only those who are yet completely men are in danger."

"Do not do this, Juan Manuel. For the memory of what I once was—what we all were. . . . But I will tell you about the courage. I left my gonads in Torreón, I left them in Zacatecas—oh, I did not know it then, but every cam-

14

paign took a little from me—and I finally lost them at Celaya. Yes, at Celaya I finally recognized the fact that I was no longer young. It is a terrible thing to grow old in the midst of great futility. It was my destiny to be old when the thing started. A man should grow old strongly —old age should be a positive sort of thing, not anything like this. And yet, believe me, Juan Manuel, you too, will grow old. That is, I suppose, what makes it bearable in the end. Things have a way to equalize themselves. When I went to war, I was three times as old as you, and now I am only twice as old. Think of it, Juan Manuel, you are gaining on me. You will be me someday."

Repentant and ashamed, Juan Rubio spoke to the old soldier. "I am sorry, believe me. It is only that I remembered the old times, which are really not so old after all. Forgive me, old one, for I have loved you, and love you now. But do not think you are as soft as you make out to be. If a man has been a man, he will always be a man. I know I will be. I will never forget that which I believe is right. There must be a sense of honor or a man will have no dignity, and without the dignity a man is incomplete. I will always be a man."

"Ojalá," said the General.

"For the present," said Juan Rubio, "I will run cattle for your gringo, but only because I would rather do that than work as a farmhand. After all, I am a jinete."

"Good," said the General. "Let us go in and join the others until you leave. My wife will be happy to see you again. Meanwhile, I will make a report of your escape in which I will give you a false name and a fantastic description."

"The teniente who arrested me knows my name," said Juan. "Will he not talk?"

"By noon tomorrow, he will be the youngest captain in this new National Army of México."

II

Thus Juan Rubio became a part of the great exodus that came of the Mexican Revolution. By the hundreds they crossed the Río Grande, and then by the thousands. They came first to Juárez, where the price of the three-minute tram ride would take them into El Paso del Norte —or a short walk through the open door would deposit them in Utopia. The ever-increasing army of people swarmed across while the border remained open, fleeing from squalor and oppression. But they could not flee reality, and the Texans, who welcomed them as a blessing because there were miles of cotton to be harvested, had never really forgotten the Alamo. The certain degree of dignity the Mexicans yet retained made some of them turn around and walk back into the hell they had left. Others huddled close to the international bridge and established a colony on the American side of the river, in the city of El Paso, because they could gaze at their homeland a few yards away whenever the impulse struck them. The bewildered people came on—insensitive to the fact that even though they were not stopped, they were not really wanted. It was the ancient quest for El Dorado, and so they moved onward, west to New Mexico and Arizona and California, and as they moved, they planted their new seed.

In a dry creekbed under a trestle in Isleta, a young boy held a lantern against the dark night while four men played at cards on an old blanket.

"Call me René," said one of the men. "It is simply René. There is no need to tell more, for to tell more may mean my death."

Juan Rubio shuffled the cards and did not speak. A second man, younger than the others, spoke.

"I know you," he said. "I have seen you before."

"You know me?" asked René, a look of fear momentarily crossing his face.

"In my village it was—in Guanajuanto—when I was but a boy," continued the young man. "But I do not know your name, for I was no bigger than the boy there at the time."

"His name is not René," said the fourth man. "And you are younger than I thought to have been a soldier, for my boy there is but twelve years old and he was born before the war."

René shifted his position, as if preparing to flee when the time came. "Why do you say that," he asked, "about René not being my name?"

"Because I have seen you many times, although you took no notice of me. I saw you in the state of Aguascalientes and in other states also, but mostly in the state of Aguascalientes. You were a civilian traveling with the army—and I especially remember you because I always meant to ask you a few questions, such as which side we were on during a particular campaign, for I could never quite figure out who I was fighting for. First I was for the people, and then I was for the government, because my General Carrillo said so, and then I again was for the people, and so on. You were always with the General in those days, and I felt you could give me the answers to my questions. I took no stock in the tales of the men that you were sleeping with the General. I only felt that you had much influence and were an educated one."

"You are mistaken," said René. "It was someone else." But he was angry and his words were said in anger.

"Since you do not wish it, I will tell no one your name," said the other. "You need not fear that I will do so, but I am not mistaken, for I traveled with you, although I was but a foot soldier and you traveled with the cavalry and the General."

"I am not afraid," said René, "for I have nothing to hide. It is only that the people with whom I cast my lot are now in disfavor. It could easily have been very different, and I would be in the capital tonight, instead of here in this miserable hole."

Juan Rubio spoke up for the first time. "There is no need for you to remain here if you do not like it." He laughed, although men like René displeased him. "You know you can go to New York, or even Paris, or London. You have our permission."

René did not laugh. "You joke, Señor Rubio," he said. "But it is really no laughing matter. Here we know each other by name because we live together in common exile.

But we cannot know each other's background. I know yours because it was my business to know such things. This man knows me because, in truth, he has seen me. I was a journalist—or, rather, an expert on political matters. I am also a student of the psychology of men."

"All those things," said Juan Rubio, "in so short a lifetime you were."

"All those things," said René. "And I have been to New York and Paris and London—earlier—in my student days."

"I laugh again, Gachupín," said Juan Rubio, "at the importance you give all these things."

René's tone became noticeably boastful. "And I am also a maker of generals—I, too, had a general in the palm of my hand. He was a small cacique in a remote village, and I personally made him into a leader of men. I found Juan Carrillo when he was on a drunken spree, for he had sold a cow—where he got it I do not know—but he had money that day and was drinking and whoring, and I recognized him as exactly the kind of man I was looking for. He was a born leader without a sense of direction—brave, loyal, gullible, and cruel. He was vain as an adolescent, and he loved to drink and screw. I took him and made him into a powerful man, and he did everything I asked him to do. . . . Of course, in this I had to be careful, for he would have had me shot in a minute if he suspected that I was really doing his thinking for him. And I wrote him up in newspapers and periodicals. In the end, alas, luck, which is such a necessary thing in these matters, deserted us and he died. If this had not happened, we would be in México now, Juan Carrillo and I, for I had decided that he should support Obregón."

"He was but a small shit," said Juan Rubio with contempt. "Shot by a woman—a grown man who allowed his balls to be shot clean away from his body. What a fitting end for someone like him."

"My one mistake," said René, "was to allow women to follow the troops. Women are always trouble—I myself have never really needed one—but Juan taught them to

18

shoot, and a gun in their hand was as deadly as one in the hand of a man."

"He was nothing, and thus you are nothing," said Juan Rubio.

René looked down and away from Juan Rubio's face. Unaccountably, he had tried to impress this man and had failed. Somehow, he could now see his failure in the manner the other meant. He picked up the cards and began to deal. Preoccupied as he was with thoughts of what might have been, he was suddenly aware that the stakes had increased and that in a minute he would win everything.

The boy holding the lantern suddenly put it out. Juan Rubio reached toward the money and grasped a man's wrist strongly. A shot rang out in the dark, and it was not necessary for him to hold the wrist, for the man fell over on his face on the money. When the lamp was lighted once again, the boy was huddled against a support of the bridge and his father lay dead on the money. René put his gun away and Juan Rubio said:

"You need not have shot him."

"He was a thief," said René.

"He was that—and a fool also—but he need not have died," said Juan Rubio. "Are your fears so great that you must kill all who once knew your name? Take your money and go far; I will take him to his woman." He looked at the man who had been in the ranks of the army of Carrillo and thought of the ignobleness of death.

The man who died under the bridge that night had no name. Who he was, where he came from, how he lived— these things did not matter, for there were thousands like him at this time. This particular man had fought in the army of General Carrillo, who, in turn, was one of the many generals in the Revolution. And, like thousands of unknown soldiers before and after him, this man did not reason, did not know, had but a vague idea of his battle. Eventually there was peace, or a lull in the fighting, and he escaped with his wife and children and crossed the border to the north. Then he took his family to Pecos, far into the new country, and there, on Mr. Henderson's ranch, he shared a crop and became a cotton farmer.

19

He had a house there in which to live, and corn and beans and occasionally meat. His cotton grew high, for cotton, and was one day thickly white. Mr. Henderson rode into the yard on horseback accompanied by a friend. He wore a star on his shirt.

"Eh, Señor Jéndeson," the sharecropper called, for it was now his custom to joke with his boss, "is it that now you are on the side of the law?" The rancher laughed also. "Yes, Mario," he answered. "All the big men around here are special deputies." He spoke to his companion for a moment, then pulled his rifle out of its scabbard and dropped it on the ground as they rode away.

The man Mario watched them ride away. He picked the gun up and inspected it, then leaned it against the house. Strange behavior, he thought. Doubtless the patrón would return for it.

It was nearly dark when Mr. Henderson returned. There were more men with him now, and one of them saw the rifle and brought it to a big man who was the sheriff. The sheriff spoke, and it amazed Mario that this man so far from his own country could speak Spanish. "Why did you forcibly take this gun from your patrón, peón?" he asked.

"I did no such thing," said Mario. "He himself threw it on the ground when he went away. I but put it aside, out of the way of the children, for I knew he must come back to get it."

"The man calls me a liar," said Mr. Henderson.

"Do not call a white man a liar, boy," said the sheriff.

"Do not call me a boy," said Mario, "for you cannot be much older than I am."

"You are leaving tonight," said the sheriff. "Get your family and your things together. Mr. Henderson will pay your train fare to El Paso. Be thankful."

Mario now wished he had kept the rifle out of sight. It was not difficult to see what was happening to him, but if he had the rifle, he would resist until death. He knew also that if he resisted he would surely die. "But my cotton," he said. "I have worked for almost a whole year for Mr. Jéndesen. Then, when we planted the cotton, he

20

explained it to me that half of it belongs to me. The bolls are very big now and very white."

"It is because of your attack on Mr. Henderson that you forfeit your claims. You should not have done that. Now, prepare to leave," said the sheriff. "It is useless to argue."

But this man called Mario had a few gold pieces saved from a time long ago, when a pueblo had been sacked in the central part of México. With these he gambled under the trestle in Isleta. He had a plan, this man Mario, of how to get a little more money, in order to buy a piece of land in his home state. He would return to México—of that there was no doubt—but he would return with a certain amount of money, and if he did not win it fairly, he had a plan. He gave his oldest boy his orders and set out to find the trestle where it was said men would sometimes play at cards for gold.

III

Juan Rubio worked first running cattle across the border, living with the greatest assortment of bad men he had ever known, sleeping always with one hand on his gun and the other on his knife. Whenever he had a few days free, he visited his woman in Juárez, whose name he now knew to be Dolores. She had removed herself from her old life and lived in a small white house on the river's edge. Soon she would also cross the border; but one day Juan's wife and three children arrived, making it out of the question for Dolores to come over the line. He moved his family to Isleta, and there he picked cotton and gambled and drank; occasionally, he fought. But every weekend he visited his Dolores, whom he loved until the day she told him she was pregnant.

Boredom worked its magic on the once active man. There had been no word from Canutillo, the hacienda of Francisco Villa—no word of the General, in fact—and Juan knew that it was time to do something. It was his feeling that perhaps destiny had chosen him to be a part in the changing of history.

He stood with his back against the adobe wall of the warehouse building, drawing deeply on the last of his cigarette. He held the cigarette with his fingertips, the lighted end toward his palm. He wore huaraches and the white breeches of the peasant and a large hat. His sarape was worn poncho-like and his sidearm was pulled forward, hanging near his groin. He felt a mild excitement now, after months of dissatisfaction. He had been visited at night by a total stranger and had sent him away, but now here he was, ready for an appointment with the politicians, prepared to do a thing he had believed he would never do. The door to the building was a few feet away to his right. He had been standing here, watching, for nearly an hour, making himself deliberately late. It was only a moment ago that he had lighted a cigarette, for he must be certain everything was all right outside before he entered the warehouse.

So this was the way these things happened? In the dark of night, strangers meet and talk, and a thousand miles away a man would soon die. Strange witchcraft!

Juan Rubio believed in witchcraft, for he had seen many times the things the art could do, but he was also a realist, and this was not really witchcraft; hence the garments of the peasant. If he was to go south tonight, he would do it as a peón. He moved to the door and knocked, as he had been directed to do. He heard movement inside, the rasp of the bolt, and a face peered out from the darkness within.

"Is it you, Colonel?"

"To serve you," said Juan Rubio. He entered, and the door was bolted once again. When the lamp was lighted, he was standing against the door and his gun was in his hand.

"There is no need for the gun, my friend," said one of the men. He wore rimless glasses and was short and slight of body. "We are friends here, and in particular there is a man here who counts himself as a friend of yours—the Señor Soto."

Juan looked at René, who sat at one end of the table around which four other men sat. "He is not my friend," he said. "And neither are you. In fact, I doubt that you

22

are friends of each other. In all of México, you will not find two men who are truly friends." He put his gun away. "I distrust you because you are politicians and because I do not know you. I have been alone too long and must protect myself—by myself."

"I am José Luís Zamora," said the small man. "René Soto you are acquainted with, if he is not your friend. The others—I could give you names, but they are only names and unimportant. The important thing is the cause, and that is the reason we are here tonight."

"I do not know of the cause—at least in the sense you do," said Juan Rubio almost surlily. "I do not believe you and I are working toward the same end at all, but I am here because, no matter what your aim might be, the act, when accomplished, will benefit México."

"You are prepared to do it, then?" asked the small man. "Ah! You are a true patriot to agree to such a task before we quote a price."

"Did I not tell you?" said René Soto.

Juan Rubio spoke to the group, but his words were directed at René. "I want you to understand—every one of you—that I am not a man to do things in this way. I agree to do it only because I please, and not because you have convinced me to do it, nor because you control me. I follow but one man, and after him no one. You have no claims on me now, nor will you have claims on me if I live after the deed is done. I will kill you your President only because there are many reasons why he should die. But I am a soldier, and am neither a politician nor a fanatic—small difference in the two in these times—and I cannot forget that I have always faced my man openly."

The small man spoke, and there was a sharpness in his voice. "Your attitude is not what we want for a task such as this one we propose. You are too arrogant, my friend, and your arrogance constitutes a danger to our plan. Other men are involved and their blood would run free, I fear, if we were to assign this job to you. Perhaps we have made an error, or the voice of Señor Soto has been overly persuasive."

"I resent that strongly, José Luís," said René, standing

23

suddenly. "I have told you this is the man, and I still believe he is the man. I *know* men—I have been in these things many years, and I know of what I speak. It would be suicidal to entrust this task to a zealot! The man to carry this out must be cool and calculating, and he must be allowed to proceed in this as he pleases. He must be a patriot, and I assure you Juan Manuel Rubio is a patriot—but he must also have personal reasons burning deep within him."

"I desire but one thing," said Juan Rubio, "and that is the name of a man in the capital who can find me a place in which to hide for a day or two. Other arrangements I will make myself. I want no money."

René spoke to the little man. "We have no choice, José Luís. And we are fortunate that our only choice is the best we could have made."

The little man put his face in his hands, his elbows on the table. "I do not know," he said. "I truly do not know."

"A spirited horse must be given his head," said René.

José Luís Zamora threw up his hands in a gesture of resignation. "If the other gentlemen are agreed," he said, "I accept him also."

"The analogy of the horse," said Juan Rubio to René. "It is well put. You are thinking, of course, that a spirited horse *can* be controlled."

René looked directly at Juan Rubio's face. "Yes, I am, don Juan."

"Take such ideas out of your head," said Juan Rubio, with a smile. "For to control a strong beast a man must first have a strong hand. And there is another gamble you take, René—I may die before the week is out."

"It is good we understand each other," said René, through lips that barely moved.

There was a knock on the door, and the lamp was turned down. Juan Rubio once again had his gun out as the door was opened and a man came violently into the room.

"It has happened, señores," the new voice cried excitedly before the lamp had been turned up. "The General is no more! Pancho Villa is dead!"

24

Juan stood with his arms hanging limply at his sides, his gun dangling from his hand. His face was pale, and he said that which he knew was not true. "You lie, son of a bitch! You lie! I do not know your motives, but you lie!"

"The details, man," said Zamora. "Quickly!"

"It was in his automobile that it happened, as his car crossed a gully. Stationary machine guns set off a crossfire, and it is a miracle if any of the men with him escaped," said the messenger. "His body is en route to the capital this minute, and will be shown to the people at the Zócalo. The news was kept from coming north, and very effectively. The atrocity was committed this morning, and we heard rumors on the other side this afternoon, but we waited to be certain."

"It is true, then?" asked René. "It cannot possibly be propaganda—I am a newspaperman and know the powers of the propaganda."

"It is true. I myself saw the marconigram from Chihuahua just this moment," said the messenger.

"Then we are finished," said René. "Our work here is done, my friends, for we have lost the one man who could have taken the ragged and the hungry, the lame—and, yes, even the blind into the fight once more. The people would do for that man that which they would do for no other. And he was a brute . . . but what a magnificent one! History is replete with men like him—one to a generation—and none greater than he was."

Zamora paced back and forth. "Do not listen to this man, señores. That of the poet and the romantic within him is but showing itself. The man Villa was needed, to be sure, but he was not absolutely essential. His death will slow us a little, but he was expendable—not as expendable as most men, perhaps, but expendable nevertheless. We must search for another crude, vulgar leader for the masses. Vainglorious, dull, and malleable. We have the makings of such a man right in this room—but then we cannot send him to México."

And Juan Rubio was apart from them, rocking in his grief. He was on his knees, holding his head in his hands, and he cried unrestrainedly, as a child would cry. And as

25

he cried he was afraid, and this was the first time; for although he had known fear, it had been momentary, and this was an intelligent fear, for himself and for humanity, but mainly for himself. The death of an immortal showed most clearly the unalterable fact that everyone must die, himself included. He had never really believed this before now. But his grief was as short as it was intense, and from now on there would be an ache and an emptiness and occasionally a dull moan, but this thing was over and in a sense he was free. He stood once again, and his dignity was noticeable, as if regenerated by the purge of his tears.

"Forgive me," he said, "but I did not hear what you were saying. But then I am not interested. I will go now, for I want nothing to do with the likes of you."

"Wait, wait!" said Zamora. "That of the trip to México is, of course, out of the question now, but we have other plans for you."

"Forget your plans," said Juan Rubio. "I want no part of them." He was impatient and was becoming visibly angry.

René Soto moved to his side. "Accept my deepest sympathies, don Juan," he said. "I know what the General was to you—what he was to your people. And, believe me, I, too, want no part of what these men will propose."

"Thank you," said Juan. "Let me move."

But Zamora stood at the door, a halfsmile on his face, and began to speak almost indulgently to Juan Rubio. "Colonel," he said, "you claim to be a soldier and a fighter for the people. You loved your general and now he is dead, and those responsible for his death are ruling your people. It is not fitting that a man such as you should simply forget this and walk away."

"Forget!" shouted Juan Rubio. "Is this capón insane? Forget!" He moved toward Zamora. "You say *forget*, you stupid bastard. Of course I will not forget! But for the moment I can do nothing. A time will come when I will do that which you wanted me to do, and when I am finished, if I live I will put the gun away forever. I will do it when he is relaxed with success. It may be five years or it may be ten, but I will get him even if it is twenty years. You may be sure he will be there twenty years, for he considers the nation his. Until that day, I will live in peace. I have been a gun fighter too long—much too long—and I have been fortunate and I have killed many times. I was fifteen the first time, and now I have twenty-seven years and have had my fill for the present." His anger was checked now, and he continued, in a sarcastic mood, "Forget, you say! Can I forget while I am looking at people like you? Can I possibly forget while you speak to me as if I were a child? I do not like that, Zamora. Do not make that mistake again. You are being dishonest with me, but I was dishonest with you also. I agreed to assassinate Obregón with the hope in my heart that when Villa arose once again, he would take politicians and connivers such as you and make them dig their own graves. We did it in Torreón, you know. We took the Chinese and the Spaniards and killed them in bunches, and everyone said we were massacring chinitos and gachupines simply because of their nationality, and the truth was that we did it because we could not trust them. They would have inherited the city we liberated, and someday we would have to return and fight for it again. That is the only way to save México, by killing all leeches such as you. All this because there is no one left whom we can trust. But it was not to be so. The destiny said no to me, so I go now."

Zamora started to speak once more. "You can have power, man. And riches . . ."

René Soto grabbed him by the lapels of his jacket. "Do you not see, José Luís, this man is truly an idealist? Perhaps the first such person I have seen in my life, and I tell you his kind are dangerous! Do you want a massacre in this room? You will have just that if you insist!" He turned to Juan Rubio and said, "Let us go, Colonel. I want to go with you."

"Stop patronizing me, for Christ's sake. Call me Juan. I am not an idiot."

Outside in the darkness, René said, "To México, I suppose."

"Are you crazy, too? Juárez is full of government spies

27

by now. I would not get two blocks into the country—in fact, I must leave El Paso as soon as possible. It is not safe for me here."

"I have always held the desire to visit the state of California," said René.

"I have never thought of California," said Juan Rubio. "But then I suppose it is as good a place as any at this time."

"You know," said René, "I have really been to Paris and London."

Juan Rubio laughed as he had not laughed for many days.

IV

In Los Angeles, he mourned deeply the loss of his god, but he was an active man and could not remain idle. Now he helped build the tall buildings, and was one day buried in a sand slide, but he survived, and soon his wife and children caught up with him once more. He found a new respect for this woman, who had relentlessly followed him so many miles, and his nurtured ego made him love her for the first time in his life. He stopped his drinking and gambling, and learned to be discreet in his love affairs. Two months later, their manchild, Richard, was born, and the mother believed that he was the reason her man had changed his wild way of life.

It was near Brawley, in the Imperial Valley, at a place where a dry creek met a tributary of the Canal del Alamo, that Richard was born. The Rubio family lived in a white clapboard house on a melon farm, on land that had been neardesert not too long ago. On one side of the habitation ran the creek, which was lined by drab mesquites and an occasional sausal. To the other side, as far as the eye could see and beyond, over the horizon, could be seen rows and rows of melons. Here and there a clump of trees shimmered, hull-down, seemingly dancing when viewed across acres of heat. The land had been reclaimed and the valley made artificially green and fertile, but the oppressive heat remained, and the people who tilled the fields, for the most part, came from the temperate climate of the central plateaus of México and found it difficult to acclimatize. Every day, one or two or three of them were carried, dehydrated and comatose, from the field, placed in some shade, and administered cold-water spongings, until, revived and more than a little nauseous, they returned to the field to close the gap in the ranks made by their departure. Indeed, there were a few that year who died before they could receive help, and were carted off to El Centro, where they ended up in a pauper's grave or on a slab in some medical school in Los Angeles or San Francisco. No one knew; and if the deceased had loved ones, they were not allowed to hold a wake, for the body belonged to the state, since there was no money to be had for a mortician, and although the people were religious, their poverty made them practical, and what little money they gathered was used to keep the living alive. So in the two or three hours it took for the authorities to arrive in the ominous gray hearse, the bereaved paid their last respects and devotion to the departed soul, worshiped the body until the hearse arrived, and the hot air was filled with anguished screams.

Then the people began to bury their own dead, in the age-old custom of people, and the only person who knew the location of the unmarked graves was an agnostic who had been a novice in a seminary in Guadalajara and who was also the only person who could lead the people in prayer in the manner in which they were accustomed. The emigrants were scattered throughout the valley, and it was a hardship to visit each other, yet they somehow formed a unit of society, and they kept its secrets well—so well, in fact, that when a witch was murdered (for there were witches in those days, as there are today), she was committed to the earth, and the English-speaking population knew nothing of her death, if, indeed, they had known of her existence.

It was here, then, near Brawley one night after she had fed her family that Consuelo Rubio felt the urge to urinate. The outhouse was near the bank of the creek under one of the willows, and she took a coal-oil lamp, for there was no wind. It was cool, as it is at night in the desert, and she wrapped her shawl around her shoulders and stepped outside. She took a few steps, and suddenly she did not know where she was going, or for what reason she was outside the house. She looked at the lamp in her hand for a long moment, then set it on the ground and wandered aimlessly. Now she walked on the creekbed, first on gravel, and the sound her shoes made on the pebbles penetrated her senses, and in her mind she was back on the hacienda in Zacatecas, walking on a dry creekbed such as this, although she did not know she was on a creekbed, on her way to a manantial for water. She reached a sandy stretch and walked on, and she was dangerously near the bank of the canal. The urge to urinate, which had left her, returned with an intensity she could not resist, and she undid her cotton drawers and squatted, holding the folds of her dress under her armpits. And there on the soft sand she dropped her child. She remained in that position, draining, and did not hear her husband, who, suddenly realizing she had but a few days before her confinement, left the house to see that she did not stumble or in some way injure herself. He picked the lamp up and called to her, and he would not have found her except for the fact that somehow she got the baby to breathe and a child's cry is unmistakable. He found her then, still sitting as she had delivered, an end of her shawl around the child, her mind still distracted. Slowly he set the lamp down, and tenderly he picked his woman and child up and carried them to the house.

"Your mother has given light," he said to his oldest daughter. "Go to the creekbed and bring the lamp and cover up the mess with sand."

He was very nearly overcome by emotion, and did not question the strangeness of this as he gently laid his wife on the bed. He wiped the placenta off her ankles and feet with the shawl, while another daughter brought him warm water with which to clean the child. He had never been this close to the birth of a child, for men are usually removed from such things, but he had seen animals foal, and he took his pocketknife and severed the umbilical cord. A woman from another house came then, but before he gave her the child, he realized he did not know its sex, and now he cried, not because it was a manchild, or because its genitalia seemed enormous in proportion to the little body, but because he was relaxed and because for a moment he had caught a glimpse of the cycle of life, lucidly not penumbrally, and he knew love and he knew also that all this was good.

He took a shovel and walked to the creek to deeper bury the afterbirth, for he had a dread that a stray dog would be attracted and eat his blood.

The nomadic pace increased. Lettuce harvests in Salinas, melons in Brawley, grapes in Parlier, oranges in Ontario, cotton in Firebaugh—and, finally, Santa Clara, the prune country. And because this place was pleasing to the eye, or because they were tired of their endless migration, Juan Rubio and his wife settled here to raise their children. And, remembering his country, Juan thought that his distant cousin, the great General Zapata, had been right when, in speaking of Juan, he once said to Villa, 'He will go far, that relative of mine.'

Now this man who had lived by the gun all his adult life would sit on his haunches under the prune trees, rubbing his sore knees, and think, *Next year we will have enough money and we will return to our country.* But deep within he knew he was one of the lost ones. And as the years passed him by and his children multiplied and grew, the chant increased in volume and rate until it became a staccato NEXT YEAR! NEXT YEAR!

And the chains were incrementally heavier on his heart.

TWO

It was spring in Santa Clara. The empty lots were green with new grass, and at the edge of town, where the orchards began their indiscernible rise to the end of the valley floor and halfway up the foothills of the Diablo Range, the ground was blanketed with cherry blossoms, which, nudged from their perch by a clean, soft breeze, floated down like gentle snow. A child walked through an empty lot, not looking back, for the wake of trampled grass he created made him sad. A mild, almost tangible wind caressed his face and hair like a mother's hands, washing him clean as it fondled him and passed to who knows where. Suddenly a jack rabbit, startled by his unseen presence, leaped past his feet and bounded across the city street, and meanwhile the multicolored birds blended, lending their opulence to the scene. His every sense responded to life around him. He thought the robin and the rabbit were God's favorites, because they were endowed with the ability to make play out of life. And, as young as he was, things were too complex for him.

The small boy was on his way home from his first confession. In one hand he carried a brand-new cap; in the other a small picture of the Virgin Mary, in a gilt-edged frame. The object, of itself, had little value for him, but he had wrapped it in his handkerchief to protect it, because he had won it by being the first in his age group to learn the catechism and, as his first symbol of recognition, it gave him a pleasant feeling. He walked diagonally across an empty block, stopping now and again to listen to some sound or to inspect a green insect. Every bug he saw was green, and he idly wondered why.

Such things worried him, always. The sky was his biggest problem these days. In the beginning, there was darkness—nothing, he was told, and accepted, before God made the world.

Who made the world?

God made the world.

Who is God?

God is the Creator of Heaven and Earth and of all things.

He knew this. He did not have to think to know—like the way he knew his prayers, like the way he turned when someone called his name or the way his eye closed when a fly came near it. It had occurred to him once that the answer to the second question was nothing more than the answer to the first. That he still did not know who God was. But upon reflection he remembered that one does not question God, and was satisfied.

But if there was nothing at the beginning, what was there? Just a big bunch of empty sky? But if it was even just empty sky, it was *something!* And the darkness! Was not the darkness *something?*

Someday he would ask, when he could ask it without getting all mixed up; he was certain someone would tell him.

He stopped in the shade of a giant oak that grew in the center of the field, and thought how wonderful it was that birds were able to fly, and lived in trees, thus exposing their red breasts. If they had been made like a bug, only their ugly grayishbrown backs would be seen. When he reached the other side of the square and turned down his street, he hastily put his cap on. It would not do to have his father catch him bareheaded. Only two weeks ago his father had made him walk three miles because he had forgotten his cap. They had been out in the country gathering wood, and when the man suddenly realized the boy was bareheaded, he scolded him and sent him home. To his father, a hat was an essential part of a man, and the boy had not imagined that it meant such a thing to him.

The red ugly building that was his home was before

33

him now. It had been a store at one time, and faded lettering was still legible on its high front. "CROCKERIES" and "SUNDRIES," it read. Below that, in smaller lettering, "Livery Stable." The "sundries" had bothered him for a long time, until finally, one day, he asked his teacher what "soondries" meant and she did not understand him. When he spelled the word out for her, she laughed and told him it meant "a great many things." She then taught him to pronounce the word. Although he liked his teacher, he never forgave her for laughing at him, and from that day he was embarrassed whenever he was corrected by anyone. And when he daydreamed in class and she asked, in exasperation, "Richard, of what are you thinking?" he answered, "Sundries." He waited patiently for the day he would run across the word when reading aloud in class, and when that day came, it was before a different teacher, and instead of the elation he had anticipated, he was left with a curious dissatisfaction. Now, as he stood before his house, he pronounced the word almost soundlessly. He was afraid of being caught talking to himself.

He walked into the house and heard his mother singing in the kitchen. In a clear, fine voice, she sang ballads of the old days in her country, and the child was always caught in their magic. He was totally unaware that his imaginary remembrances, being free of pathos, were far more beautiful than her real ones.

"You are home, my son?" she asked.

"Sí, Mamá." He kissed her and then handed her the small picture. "Here. It is my prize."

"Ah! What a good son you are. Your father will be proud." She kissed him again. "Now, change your clothes. You must save these for school."

"Yes, but first I must ask you something."

She stopped suddenly as she was turning from him. She had an instinctive fear of her son's questions, for she sensed that although he was but nine years old, he would soon ask her things she did not discuss even with her husband. She looked at him. His dark face was cupped in his frail hands, and his thin elbows rested on the table. His face was a miniature replica of hers. High cheekbones, small chin, black eyes; the nose was long, and it hooked down at the tip, exactly as hers did. Only his ear lobes were different. They were extraordinarily large, like her husband's. His fingers were long and nervous.

All indio, this boy of mine, she thought, except inside. The Spanish blood is deep within him.

She was concerned for this child of her heart. Eight girls she had borne in her thirty-four years, and this was her only son. He had brought her and her man back together, and for that she could never love him enough. But he was such a rare one! Her face softened and she said:

"Very well, son. What is it that you want to know?"

He turned a perplexed face to her. "The good Father asked me some strange things today, Mamá," he said.

"Is that what you want to talk about?" she asked, and her voice showed gentle reproof. "You know it is a sin to discuss a Holy Confession with anyone." She prepared to dismiss him, thankful for the opportunity.

He spoke again, before she could say another word. "He asked me if I liked to play with myself, and I said yes, and he was angry." With his limited knowledge of English, the translation into Spanish was a literal one, and she did not fully understand his meaning. "I could not say no, because it is true that I would rather be alone than with the Portuguese and the Spaniards. They always hit me, anyway, and make fun of me. Tell me, why should I play with the others if they do not like me?"

She would not try to explain to him the importance of companionship and the security of belonging to a group. It would only make her think of how she herself was sometimes lonely here without any of her people. "Talk to your father later. He will tell you," she said. "Now, go do what I told you."

"There is more, Mamá. He asked me also if I sometimes play with Luz. You yourself make me play with her, so I answered yes. Then he wanted to know if I ever touch her, and I said I do, and he was angrier. After a while, his voice was kind and he told me it is a mortal sin to touch a girl, and even worse to touch your own sister. I never knew that one mortal sin could be worse than another mortal

35

sin. Fifty Our Fathers and fifty Hail Marys he gave me to say for penance."

The full meaning of what he was saying struck her so she perceptibly shrank from him. What can I say? she thought. How can I tell him? Near panic, she started to refer him to his father again, but he said:

"I know what he meant about touching Luz. I did not remember before, but right now I know."

She grasped the table for support. ¡Por Diós! she thought. He knows all about being with a woman! Her face was white, and she hoarsely whispered through her teeth, "Tell me how you know what he meant! Tell me now!"

"It is nothing," he said quietly, but her vehemence frightened him. "It happened so long ago I had forgotten—and I do not see why it is a mortal sin."

"A long time ago!" The initial shock was past, and she was at the point of violent anger. "What happened a long time ago? What did you do? Tell me!"

He could not understand the reason for her wrath. "You remember the Mangini girls when I was little and we lived in the other house? You liked them because they were good to me and always took me with them when they went out into the empty lots to get milkweed for their rabbits. When we were out in the fields, they took my trousers off and played with my palomas and laughed and laughed. Then they took their clothes off, and hugged me and rolled around in the grass. And they would say they wished I was older but if I was older they could not play with me like that. And you know? The big ones had hair on their body, except that one of them had only a little bit."

"Pig! Pig! Ah, what has God given me? A shameless!"

He continued in a calm voice, now seemingly apathetic to her fury, "And then, one day, the girls were starting to get dressed when the biggest one grabbed me, and she started to moan like she was crying, and she bit me on the shoulder and made me cry. I never went out with them again."

"Why did you not tell me of this before?" she shouted.

"They told me it was our secret, and they bought me ice-cream cones if I promised not to tell anyone." He paused a moment. "I guess that is what the priest meant. Now I will have to make another confession, because I have never played like that with Luz and I told him I did. And I think I did not say all my penance—I lost count."

"You are bad! Filthy!" She pushed him roughly into the large room that was the bedroom for the whole family. "Tomorrow, early, you go to confession and tell all that to the Father. Now you better pray that you do not die tonight!" She sat at the table and, with her head on her arms, began to cry.

The frightened and bewildered boy sat on the bed where four of his sisters slept. He took off his clothes, crying silently. As his sobs subsided, he wondered why his parents, who were so good to him, could change so suddenly to become almost vicious. The very bed he sat on was an example of their goodness, for they preferred to sleep on the floor so that their children could have it. There was something here that he did not know. A mystery so great that it could not be spoken about, so great that it could only be mentioned indirectly. Why did they not want to tell him? *God made the world. Who is God?* But if He was good and kind, why did He make darkness? Night was the scariest time of the day, because a day is twenty-four hours and night is a day. But not daytime. He was scared at night because he could not see, and he was frightened now because he could not know, and somehow God was in the middle of the whole thing. To do "bad" things had something to do with being alive, but really what were "bad" things? As he thought, he almost marveled, because experiences that had left him shaken and afraid were nearly always somehow connected with the mystery. It seemed years ago that he had sat on a box at an old squeaky table under the prune trees. Across from him, his father sat eating his food. His sisters sat around the table on both sides of them. They were eating, too, but he could not eat. He just sat there staring at his frijoles, and all the time his stomach kept bothering him, just as it did when he took castor oil. He felt the corner of his mouth jerk down, but he could not cry. Not yet. He could hear the little animals chirping and making noises in the darkness

37

around him. The little boys from the other families were playing hangolseek in the orchard, stepping all over the fruit, probably. Once in a while, a prune would fall from the limb on top of him and make a funny little noise when it hit the table. He used to like that before, because once one fell on his father's plate and he got mad, but now he did not feel good. He looked up when his father spoke in a strong voice:

"Eat! Are we so rich that our food can be thrown away?"

"No, Papá. It is only that I don't feel good. I am worried about my mother."

"Do not worry, son." He did not sound mean this time. "Your mother is all right. Go in and see her if you wish. Give me your plate. I will finish it myself."

"Sí, señor," he said, and jumped off the box. He opened the flap of the tent, and now he wanted to turn back. His mother was making terrible noises. Funny he had not heard her moaning when he was outside. He could not turn back, and he really wanted to, because he was scared. There was a dirty old blanket that his father had put across the middle of the tent so they would not bother Mamá. They all slept in the tent—his six sisters, too—and Papá wanted to be sure they would not bother Mamá. He got down like a little cat and crept under the blanket, and then he kneeled down next to his mother. She stopped moaning for a little while and she was sweating. In her hands she had her rosary beads, the good ones. His uncle Juan had given them to her when she married his father. His uncle had just come back from walking like a little cat all the way to the shrine of the Dark Virgin, almost eight leagues away, and he felt very good inside. So he gave her his rosary. Everyone said that that was a bad sign, to give your own rosary beads away, but his uncle Juan just laughed and drank more tequila. He died the next day. He just got a pain and died. Richard knew the story; his father had told him about it over and over.

His mother's lips were very wet when he kissed her, and they did not smell too good.

"¿Cómo está, Mamá?" he started to ask. She turned

38

her face, and her eyes were not there for him. It looked like she was looking right through him, but when she talked, she talked to him and nobody else.

"I am all right, little one." She talked like she was very tired. "The Virgin is looking out for me."

He wanted to holler out against the Lord and the Virgin for making her suffer, but he got scared and crossed himself because he had a bad thought. He lied to his mother. "I ate all my food, Mamacita, but the tortillas were not like you make them. You make them much better."

She said, "That is good, son. Now, go outside for a while." But when she said that, she gave a big yell and pulled her hands apart. The rosary beads broke, and part of them fell to the dirt floor. He looked at her face and his body was very cold, and he could not move, but then he jumped up and ran out, shouting, "My mother is dying! My mother is dying, and it's my fault. I thought against God, and the rosary broke! It's the sign! She is going to die, and it's my fault—my fault—my grievous fault!"

Everybody ran around and left him by himself, so he fell on his stomach and cried very hard and his face got dirty. After a while, he stopped crying. His mother was shouting so much that he could even hear her outside. He walked away into the orchard. He began to think.

Maybe it isn't my fault, he thought. Maybe Mamá got bit by a little animal. But when he thought of that, he got scared all over again, because only last week Papá had caught him playing with a little animal that had a red stomach. He had been poking it with a stick and Papá stepped on it and took his stick away from him and hit him with it, because he said that the animal would kill him. After a while, he had asked his father how a funny little animal with a red stomach could kill him, and he answered that it would bite him and he would just swell up and die. He remembered that when he went in to see his mother, she was all swelled up. He ran back to the tent, and went inside to the corner where his mattress of potato sacks was, and stood there on his knees praying. He said more than ten Hail Marys and Our Fathers, and then began to make up his own prayers. He promised Him so

39

many things that he could not remember, and all the time his mother kept screaming, and his father came to him and fell asleep on his mattress of potato sacks like nothing was happening. He wanted to sleep, too, as his father was doing, but he could not. Instead of trying to sleep some more, he finally got a coal-oil lamp and lit it. He tried to read from his book, *Toby Tyler, or Ten weeks with the circus.* He would never forget the name of it, because he liked it so much and had read it five times before. His teacher in Brawley had given it to him, once when he went to school for about a month, and told him he should keep it until he learned to read. He read the same page over two times, and put the book away in his hiding place, because once he put it under his mattress and his baby sister wet all over it; that was why the pages were bumpy and hard. All this time, his mother kept hollering, until he thought he would bust before she did. Pretty soon, his oldest sister came and waked his father, and he went behind the blanket with her. And pretty soon his mother was quiet, and he stood there waiting, but he did not know what he was waiting for. There was one more cry, and that one was different; that was not his mother. All at once, he felt good again and knew that he could go to sleep. He forgot about God and lay down. His mother was all right. He was sure of it. Maybe he was as sure of that as he was that in a couple of days his mother would be out in the orchard picking prunes with the rest of them.

Very clearly he now knew this was a part of the mystery. He could look back to that time with the sophistication of his nine years. Since that first time, he had seen his mother big with child twice, and each time remembered the horrible fantasy of the black widow spider. So she *must* know, she had to know, and of course as long as *she* knew, it could not be too evil—and yet how did she find out? He was certain his father did not know, else he would tell him. Somehow his mother and the priest were a part of this thing that was such evil. . . . But if he had done such a great wrong, why was it that nothing had happened to him because of it? He began to cry again, because it was afternoon and it would be night soon and his punishment would come at night. He knew that bad things happen in the dark. He had not made a good confession, and he might indeed die in the night and go to Hell. *The third day He rose again from the dead.* Do many people go to Hell? He knew a boy who went to Hell, although he had never thought of this before. And he also knew that the boy was in Hell because of something having to do with the Sin. Suddenly he very nearly had the answer to the whole thing, and he was calm. Now he could remember other times the Sin had come up. . . . They told them that it was just a feeling and that they were too little to get it yet. It was nighttime almost, and the big guys were standing by the gas station talking. They were going to a hookshop, they said, and he and Ricky wanted to know what it was. The big guys laughed at them, because they were little kids and did not know nothing, and they were smarter. One of the big guys was always mean to him, because he was Spanish and Richard was Mexican. . . . He had asked him one day why he was always picking on him, and he told him because he was Mexican and everybody knew that a Spaniard was better than a Mexican any old day, and Richard told him that his father said that in Spain if a guy had a burro, he was a king; but he did not know what Richard was talking about. Richard did not stand too close to him, because he was always trying to pants him, and he would have died of shame if he did it tonight, because he knew his BVDs were dirty at the trapdoor. The boy talked louder than any of the others, and kept saying, "Let's go—I got ants in my pants," and all that, and he kept walking back and forth and holding the front of his pants with both hands. He was pretty dumb, and he was the one that got drowned in the river one time his folks went up to Sacramento to work in the asparagus. He kept hollering, "Let's go," but they had to wait for the guy with the car, and then he told Richard to get the hell away from there, cholo, because they did not want any chilebeans hanging around. Richard did not go, but he watched and was ready to start running, but the other did not chase him. Instead, he started saying things to him to make everybody laugh, like "Why don't you go home and eat some tortillas," and Richard told him he had just finished eating, and anyway he did not see anything funny about it, because he liked tortillas better than bread any old day. But it was funny to the rest of them, except Ricky, because he used to eat over Richard's house all the time. And then the guy asked him to go home and listen to the radio, although he knew Richard's family did not even have electric lights. And that was not funny either, but they kept laughing and saying all kinds of dingy things, and then the same guy told Richard to go tell his sister Concha he wanted to fuck with her. And everybody laughed louder and almost died laughing, and Richard did not know what to say, because he did not really know what the guy meant, but he did know it was bad, and he got mad and started to cry and told the guy that someday he was going to grow up bigger and beat him up. But the guy said again to call her and tell her what he said, and Richard told him that he was going to tell his father on him, and the guy said to go ahead and call him and he'd give the old bastard a highster in the ass, and everybody laughed some more and he chased him, but only a little way. They laughed at Richard's father, but they did not know about him.

II

At this time, Richard's most enjoyable moments were those spent in the company of his father. He loved his mother. She was always there when he needed her, and her arms and her songs were warmth and comfort and security, but with his father it was a different thing, because pleasure is far different from security. And suddenly he began to look forward to the time his father would return from work. Whenever possible, Juan Rubio took him with him in his travels around the valley. There were not many Mexican people in Santa Clara in those days, and the few families scattered throughout the far reaches of the valley became close friends. It was another thing in the summer, when people arrived by the hundreds from southern California, first for the apricot and then the prune harvest; but in the remaining months it was not an

42

easy thing for the people to have intercourse with someone from their own country.

With his father, Richard sat around campfires or in strange kitchens, with wood stoves burning strongly and the ever-present odor of a pot of pink beans boiling, freshly cooked tortillas filling the close, warm room, and listened to the tales of that strange country which seemed to him a land so distant, and the stories also seemed of long, long ago. It was then, listening and weaving a parallel fantasy in his mind, that he felt an enjoyment so great that he knew he could not possibly savor it all. He listened to the men speak until he grew drowsy, and he climbed onto his father's lap, and Juan Rubio held him easily against his body, close to his chest, and the boy associated the smell of the man with his happiness.

In the summer also now, it became the custom for his father to allow two or three families to pitch their tents in the large back yard, or to use a portion of the barn to live in until the prune season was over and they would return to their own part of the state. And so Richard had Mexican friends and learned more about them from living with them. They held small Mexican fiestas and sang Mexican songs, and danced typical dances, so that there, in the center of Santa Clara, a small piece of México was contained within the fences of the lot on which Juan Rubio kept his family.

Thus the summers were glorious for Richard—marred only by an occasional happening of life that is intrinsically sad, for in the Rubio yard children were born, people were married, and sometimes someone, usually a newborn baby, died. Richard could not accept the idea of death, even with the knowledge that he would go to Heaven. To die was easy, but to give up life was not an easy thing even to think about, and yet it was obvious to him that it could not be too difficult a thing, for even cowards somehow managed to die. He had seen a man die this summer, and the ease with which he had expired was frightening, and in the moment before he died there was no difference in him from the moment after he was dead—yet suddenly he was dead, irrevocably dead.

Richard was with his father talking to don Tomás that night when it happened, and don Tomás said goodnight to Juan Rubio and walked to his house in the back yard. A short time later, his stepson came over to ask for some yerba buena, because his father—he always called him his father—had a bad stomach ache. Soon he returned and asked for some alcohol to rub him down, because he was in great pain. By then, don Tomás could be heard moaning and calling to God to ease his suffering. Richard went out to the back yard to a point where he could see into the room. The bed was by the door, and it was not really dark yet, so he could see him very plainly on the bed. Don Tomás moved his head from one side to the other, and he doubled up his body with big jerks. Once, he let out a big, long fart. In the rear of the room, a candle was lighted to the Virgin and the women of the house were praying. Richard could hear the murmur all the way outside. He wanted to go into the room and look at don Tomás up close, but he was afraid he was going to die, and he did not want to watch him when he died. Juan Rubio sent him away to get the enema bag, because don Tomás kept saying he had a great constipation, but by the time he returned with the bag, his father was talking to the stepson, and the stepson got on his bicycle and went away very fast. Don Tomás did not have his conscious any more, and he was very sick, and the boy was sent to bring an ambulance. Don Tomás was quiet, lying on his back, staring at the rafters. Every once in a while, he took a deep, loud breath, and then one time he did not breathe again but kept on staring at the rafters. Juan Rubio came then and put two rocks on his eyes, and took Richard away from there. The stepson came back and said the ambulance would not come, because there was no one to pay for it, and Juan Rubio sent him back to call the cops. After a while, the Chief of Police came, and then the county hearse, gray with black curtains, came, and then an ambulance came.

The next day, they buried don Tomás, and the coroner told Juan Rubio that he had died of peritonitis, caused by a ruptured appendix, and the county buried don Tomás in the Catholic cemetery at one end near the cherry trees, because that is where the county buried people who did not have money. Juan Rubio and Richard stayed behind under the cherry trees after everybody left, and they talked because Richard was still afraid, and the boy told his father that he was afraid to die because it seemed like a big darkness and that he did not want to die ever, and his father put his arms around him, and he said that if he did not want to die ever and he wanted that very much, then he would never die. He made Richard very happy when he said that, and he believed him because his armpits smelled so nice. And then they saw that the hearse had come back to the grave. They watched them lift the coffin back out, and waited to see them throw don Tomás back in the hole and keep the coffin, but they just filled up the hole and took don Tomás away with them, coffin and all. Richard asked his father why he was crying, and Juan Rubio said that it was the only thing he could do.

That night, don Tomás returned to the back yard. An idiot girl who had runny sores, named Dora, saw him first and came running to tell everybody, and they were all frightened and closed their doors. Richard was outside under a tree when it happened, and was so frightened that he could not move and don Tomás found him there. Don Tomás looked at him sadly, and his face was very white, because he did not have any blood. He did not talk and Richard did not talk, but he knew don Tomás wanted him to put him back in his grave.

III

Near the primary school that Richard attended, there still stands a large red barn, old and abandoned, its windows boarded and its roof unshingled. Like all inutile inanimates, it gives no hint that it, too, has a past. In the early days of the motorcar, it housed the wagons and horses of one of the most successful draymen in Santa Clara. Mat Madeiros was one of those men who, being poor all their lives, become authorities on commerce and economic trends when they find themselves in the secure position of moderate wealth. Mat knew business was booming and would get even better. Soon he would not be able to handle all his orders with his modest equipment. He talked loud and long on the importance of the machine in business, and sold his horses to a farmer in Cupertino. His wagons were too heavy to be used in orchards, so he dismantled them and put them in a far corner of the barn.

Mat learned to drive his Reo truck and prospered, so that before the end of one year the vehicle was paid for, and in the second year he had visions of a fleet of trucks and an important position in the community. Every evening, he stood in front of the poolhall, sucking on a black cigar, renewing friendships with old acquaintances, thinking forward to the day he would run for the town council —he might even receive enough votes to become mayor. Gradually he became so engrossed in reveries of social accomplishment that he scarcely noticed that his hauls were becoming fewer in number. Soon his clients stopped coming altogether, and he had to drive to the neighboring towns of Berryessa, Sunnyvale, and Saratoga in search of jobs. Once, he even went all the way to Old Almaden, but to no avail. Now the household was run on the money he had saved to put into his business, and he was finally forced to work in a cannery and to put his rig up on blocks. Every evening, he went into the barn and sat at the wheel of the truck, as a child will sometimes do. With a yardstick, he measured the contents of the gas tank and then checked the tires with a handgauge, thumping each of them with the heel of his hand. Thus reassured that his truck was ready for the time hauls would begin to come up, he stood back and gave it a look of approval, then went in to his supper.

These days, Mat bolstered his spirits by declaring to his wife and children, and even to himself, that of a certainty things would soon be better. Business was bound to improve, and his rig would once again be in demand. He explained in detail how he would add more rigs and how he would have to hire a man to help out as the business grew. At the plant, he told his fellow-workers that he was there only temporarily, and because he had acquired an

46

independence when he was his own boss, he was not a good worker, and one day found himself out of a job. His small reserve had dwindled steadily and he had no money. He would not think of selling his truck, until finally, in desperation, he was forced to try, but by now he could not find a buyer. All this led to a period of notoriety for Mat's big barn.

The year was 1931, and the people of Santa Clara were hungry. The little food they could buy with their meager income was augmented only because the valley was so fertile, and now it was common practice to go into the fields and take fruits and vegetables. The smaller farmers, who could not afford to harvest their crops, willingly let the people have them. Richard's family did not suffer as much as the others, because the depression had not changed their diet. They had never had much more than they were now getting. His father had always managed to bring vegetables home to add to their basic staples. The boy was no longer greeted at noon recess with jeers and hoots. The hated, oft-repeated cries of his schoolmates— "Frijoley bomber!" "Tortilla strangler!"—now disappeared, as did the accompanying laughter, and he sometimes shared his lunch with them. He did this with a sense of triumph, because he felt he had defeated them by enduring their contempt and derision openly. For almost a year, he had purposely eaten where he could be easily observed, refusing to be driven into hiding because they laughed about the food he ate. He did not suspect the real reason for his victory.

The state of the community was reflected in the school in other ways. A new ruling made it permissible to attend classes in bare feet, and another suspended school during bad weather. The rainy-day session was a godsend to the children and, of course, defeated its purpose, for they had more time to spend on the wet streets.

The townspeople demanded help from the county, and learned that their success in this was greater if it was done collectively, rather than individually, so the Unemployed Council was born. Mat's barn was cleaned and used as a

47

meeting place and headquarters for the organization. Committees were formed to go before the Board of Supervisors, the County Welfare Department, and the mayor of Santa Clara to petition aid for the needy. And the government agencies responded as well as they possibly could. They gave commodities labeled as surplus, and distributed clothing to the worst cases. At first, the meetings were conducted in four languages—English, Spanish, Portuguese, and Italian—but as the group grew, it became increasingly difficult to maintain order. The original organizers felt that tenure should give them leadership, and refused to give the newcomers a voice. Petty jealousies were born and nurtured, until the meetings were often disrupted by violent arguments. There was soon complete demoralization, and collapse was impending, for the people had little knowledge of administrative procedure and were not overly literate. Into this chaos came the man from the city, the professional organizer.

Unemployed councils had developed in other cities throughout the state, and Communist affiliations made a concentrated effort to unite these groups into one strong structure. When the absorption of the councils was accomplished, the heretofore amicable relationship between the local groups and the authorities ended, and Mat's truck was once more on the road. Working parties forayed the bakeries for stale bread, the dairies for skim milk, and any place where they might find something to help feed the people.

Richard and his father walked into the red barn. It was different inside from the first time he had seen it. The walls were newly whitewashed and a wooden floor had been installed. At one end of the building was a raised platform on which stood a long table and several chairs. The wall behind the table was bedecked with bunting, of which a red flag with hammer and sickle was the centerpiece. This object always reminded the child of the picture on the box that held his father's indigestion medicine. The boy and his father always sat with a group of Spanish men, because, as his father said, they were not the best people with whom to associate, but they at least spoke the language of Christians. They took seats, and Richard waited for things to begin. First they would play that march on the old graphophone while everyone stood, and then they would all sing their own songs. Words had been written to the tunes of popular songs of the day and to old favorites. "Auld Lang Syne," "Home, Sweet Home," and the "Stanford Fight Song" were the most popular with the crowd. Many of these songs were simple, straightforward pleas for food and clothing, while others called on the people to rise and throw off the shackles of serfdom.

Richard had anticipated tonight with pleasure, for on this night the delegate from San Francisco came, and he always put on a performance that was better than the one-ring Mexican circus Richard once saw in Milpitas. The man would pace back and forth, at times almost falling off the platform in his enthusiasm; he would wildly wave his arms and scream in a high-pitched voice. Because he was a small man, his antics were all the more ludicrous to the boy.

The songs were now over, and the man walked toward the platform. He shook hands with everyone in his path as he made his way to the front. The local chairman said a few words of needless introduction, and the delegate began to speak. He spoke in a different voice from the one Richard knew, slowly and carefully enunciating, almost stentoriously, as if he suddenly realized that most of the assemblage had never understood a word he said.

"Comrades," he said, "the time has come for us to show the instruments of our capitalistic government that we are tired of being stepped upon. The supervisors have refused to see our committees, so from now on we will be one big committee. We are going to raise such a racket that they will not dare refuse to see us. We are hungry and will be heard. This is just the beginning of a program that will tell the world how we have been let down. If they refuse to help us, then we must redouble our efforts to help ourselves.

"And I have good news for you, Comrades—yes, good news! One day soon, people like you and I will march to

Sacramento and demand an audience with the Governor. . . . You realize what that will mean, a thing like that? People from every town and city in California, converging on the state capital? Washington will hear of it, and they will not be able to ignore us then. Plans are already in progress for the hunger march, and I personally promise you that we will make it soon. I have been assigned to remain here with you, and a Comrade will be sent to help me instruct. One day, we will have our own schools, and your children will receive the education they deserve. Now we can continue with the meeting."

He sat down amid thunderous applause, and very interestedly listened to the remainder of the meeting. Plans were made for the execution of the hunger march, and when the business at hand was out of the way, portable tables were set up and the people were served hot cocoa and bread. Many who were not local people came in to get food, and Richard watched in fascination. The men from hobo jungles interested him, because they, in spite of their obvious hunger, courteously took only one helping and withdrew, while others, whom he knew to have some food at home, returned again and again to be fed. The diverse types among these men of the road also made him curious. Some were in tatters, their dirty ankles showing between their shrunken trousers and battered shoes. There were those who wore the sturdy clothing of the farmhand and looked no different from the people of the town. There were others who, in spite of their present circumstances, still attempted to affect a manner of respectability. They wore badly wrinkled unmatched suits with chambray shirts and soiled but neatly tied neckties. Regardless of their appearance, these men all had a common, haunted look of despair. Young and old walked with the same dazed air of incomprehensibility, except the Negroes. Richard, who had never seen Negroes in his life, mistook their attitude for morbid stoicism and was frightened by the black faces. Soon, however, he easily lost himself in their laughter and horseplay, and their color lost its strange ominousness. He learned to love the amazing beauty of their wide, toothy grins. When he talked to them,

50

they told him about Alabam', the C'linas, and other such alien and mysterious places.

The next morning began a series of events that for a while kept Richard in a state of constant excitement. Always, however, there was a part of his mind that carefully observed from a detached point of view, and he was aware that he was learning something. There was a demonstration at the county courthouse in San Jose, which was in itself orderly, but the aftermath was one of spontaneous violence. What happened occurred without any apparent leadership, because the instigators kept well in the background. Food and produce trucks were marauded as they passed through town, for the old 101 highway did not bypass Santa Clara then. It was not an uncommon sight to see a truck lying on its side, with men scurrying antlike, back and forth, carrying pilfered food to their homes. Richard was often nearby, not showing his impatience, quietly calculating until he saw what he wanted. But, in spite of his careful planning, his choice of foods was bad, because he was driven by the mania of a child who had not had certain things, and by the end of the third day he had fifty loaves of bread and a hundred tins of deviled meat. He was unaware that he would have benefited had he gone about his plundering in a haphazard manner.

One Saturday morning, Richard accompanied his father to the pear groves at the north end of the valley. Although it was late in October and the Bartletts had long been harvested, the Winter Nellies were ready to be picked for shipment east. The ranchers had put out a call for workers. When Richard and his father arrived at the ranch where his father worked every season, cars were lined on both sides of the dirt driveway that led from the road to the house and the main buildings. About two hundred men were gathered in the loading area, talking quietly in small groups. Their lack of cheerfulness seemed strange to Richard, who had seen many such congregations joking and skylarking, waiting for the boss to come out. Then they would stand quietly while the strawbosses picked out the old hands, then selected the healthier-appearing and more serious of the remaining. No one would pay an hourly wage to a clown.

The steady help arrived and got to their jobs. Two men took ladders and buckets out of the big barn, while others, wearing hipboots and foul-weather clothing, coupled hoses and hitched horses to tankwagons, preparatory to spraying the Bartlett trees. Some walked into the orchard with pruning shears and saws, and others went off with axes, mattocks, and shovels to dig out dead trees.

The owner walked out then, wiping his mouth with a huge red handkerchief. Beside him was his eighteen-year-old daughter, who, since he had never had a son, kept his accounts and helped him in his business. She knew every phase of it, and would someday own one of the richest and largest orchards in the valley. She was a special friend of Richard's, for whenever his father worked there, the boy spent hours with her, and she sometimes took him into her library, where he lost himself in the books her father had bought for the son he never had.

The man and the young woman walked out to the center of the large yard. He was a good man, Mr. Jamison, and no one who had ever worked for him could say otherwise. He was not averse to taking his workers into his immaculate living room on cold mornings, where his wife would serve them hot coffee and a jigger of his good brandy. At the end of the working season, he always gave them enough wine for a party, and even got drunk in their company.

He smiled at them. "I'm sorry so many of you made an unnecessary trip out this morning," he said. "You see, I have my own packing plant and can handle only so much fruit a day, so I'm hiring only thirty men. Of course, my old help will be hired first, so those of you who've never worked for me better try somewhere else before it gets too late. If you're new in the valley, my daughter will tell you what ranches to try." No one made a move to leave, and the rancher sensed something was wrong. "What's the matter?" he asked.

None of the men who knew him would look up. An

unidentified voice called out, "What are you paying, Mr. Jamison?"

"Fifteen cents. You all know that."

"We want twenty-five, Mr. Jamison!"

The rancher shook his head in a negative gesture. "I can't do that. I'm already in trouble for paying fifteen cents, but the truth is that I just can't afford to pay more than that."

"Then your fruit'll rot, 'cause none of us will work for less'n twenty!"

The girl had been sitting on the bumper of a car talking to Richard. She got up and returned to her father's side. "Listen," she said. "Dad's telling you the truth. The Association held a special meeting last night, and we argued all night for fifteen cents. They wouldn't agree to it. . . . Twelve cents an hour is all they're paying. If you don't believe it, go see Robertson, or Black, or Genovese. Right now they're paying twelve, and the men are probably working already. Dad's offering you fifteen, the same as last year. And he'll probably get thrown out of the Growers for it."

The unidentified man spoke again. "We want twenty— or we won't work. You better make up your mind, 'cause it'll start raining soon, and then where will you be? Look at the sky. It looks like it will rain today." Someone snickered in the background. It was obvious that the man doing the talking was an outsider, for a light wind was coming in from San Francisco Bay, two miles to the north, a good indication in Santa Clara that there would be no rain.

The girl became angry then, and took a defiant step toward the approximate location of the voice.

In her blue denims and plaid shirt, her hair splashing yellow on her shoulders, her arms akimbo, she faced them, and to Richard she was the most beautiful thing he had ever seen. He did not really understand what was happening, but was in immediate sympathy with her. He moved to her side and aped her stance, and oddly his small figure was not farcical to the men.

"Just who are you?" she asked the man who had

spoken. "Step out so I can see you!" When the man did not come forward, she said, "All right! So this is a strike! We were warned that this might happen this year, but Dad wouldn't believe his friends would let him down. He's always been so good to you, and even now is doing the best he can. Do you think you're the only ones having a hard time?" She paused, then tried to reason with them; she appealed to their sense of fairness. "If that crop isn't picked, we'll be running the ranch for Giannini next year. If we pay you what you ask, we lose not only money but the ranch as well—but you don't care anything about that, do you? You forgot the things he's done for you." She was angry once more at their silence. "Cowards—you should be ashamed! Standing there without even the guts to talk, without even the guts to look squarely at us. . . . Hiding a stranger in the background to shoot off his big mouth!" She called out to them individually, talking to boys her own age, boys who had gone to school with her. "You, Mike, and Pete, and Charlie—aren't *you* ashamed of what you're doing? And you, Jack, especially you. . . . Have you forgotten, too, so soon?" And because Jack meant more to her than the others, she could be cruel to him. She spoke the bitter words brutally. "It means a lot to my old man to have his pears picked right away. Didn't it mean a lot to your folks when they got that box of groceries last week and that store order for clothing for the kids?"

"Please don't, daughter," said her father embarrassedly.

"I don't care, Pop!" She shook his hand from her arm. "Maybe I'll shame them into behaving like men." She spoke to Jack again. "You didn't know he'd done that, did you, Jack? Because he's so kind, he tried to help. Because of his goodness, he can't even be angry toward you men—if you can call yourselves men! But I'm not kind, and I'm mad! What do you think of your strike now, Jack?"

The young man was forced to speak, not only because of what she had just told him but because they had once been something special in each other's young lives, and because her father had raised her to be the kind of girl who would go with him, Jack Perreira, to the high-school senior prom. He spoke softly, almost intimately, as if the two were alone, and yet there was a hint of humility in his voice. "I knew who sent the food, Marla. I knew it right away, but now the men are striking, and no matter what I think about it and how I feel about you, I have to follow along. When you have a chance to think, you'll understand."

She did not think she could ever understand, but she somehow respected him for his words. "The offer still stands," she spoke out to the crowd. "The ladders and buckets are there for those who want to work." There was still no movement from the men. She had worked among men all her life, and knew their vernacular well. "Okay, then, you Goddamn bastards!" she shouted. "Get the hell off our property, and don't come back until you're ready to go to work. . . . And the wage has just gone down! When you come back, it'll be at twelve cents an hour. Twelve Goddamn cents is all you'll get! Right now I'm going to call the sheriff, and then I'm going to get a shotgun and shoot any son of a bitch who's still on our land and doesn't want to work." She walked to the house so rapidly that Richard was forced to run to keep up with her. Her father went off into the orchard, and the men moved their cars out to the highway. They did not trust her not to carry out her threat.

She sat under a tree, with the boy beside her and a twelvegauge shotgun across her lap, waiting for the sheriff to arrive. After a while, she sent Richard to tell the men that they were welcome to water if they were thirsty. When the sheriff and his deputies arrived, Richard stayed beside his father. Policemen frightened him, and he thought his father would be arrested. The sheriff told the men to go to work, but they ignored him. The road was public domain, and he lacked the authority to make them leave. He left his men there and moved on, for there were strikes all over the countryside.

The road where the men were keeping their vigil, although paved, was not really a highway but a county road.

55

Therefore they were surprised to see a truck, loaded with watermelons, approach and come to a stop in their midst. A lean, fairskinned young man jumped from the cab and looked around.

"Help yourself," he said casually, and walked toward an old man who was talking to Richard's father. "They told me I'd find you here," he said, and embraced the old man warmly.

"How are you, my son? How good it is to see you!" said the old man. He turned to Richard's father. "This is my son Victor, don Juan. A grown man, no?"

"Much pleasure, sir," said the young man, taking Juan Rubio's hand.

"Equally. You have come a long way, eh?"

"Imperial Valley," answered Victor. "I left two days ago and was making good time but, coño, that Pacheco Pass is more difficult than the portals of Heaven!"

"I know. I have suffered it."

The old man grabbed his son's arm. "But, man, me cago en Diós! Do you not see that those men are stealing your watermelons?" He shouted excitedly to the men, "¡Hola! ¡Marrdita sea! Take yourselves from that truck, jackoffers of the devil! Respect another's goods!" He shook his head with indignant disgust and said, "I excrete on the milk of such abusers!"

Victor laughed. "Calm yourself, old one," he said. "I told them to have some, so they would not wreck my truck. Watch how careful they are and how they do not make pigs of themselves. An old one like you should know that people behave better if they are made responsible for something." He put his hand on Richard's head and said, "Go, little one, and bring us back a good one."

They sat on a runningboard and ate the melon. A man wandered over to them and said that some of the new men had left, on the pretense of looking elsewhere for work, but had secreted themselves into the ranch by walking on a creekbed, and had been picking all along. Some of the strikers wanted to go in and drag them out, but the idea was rejected when they realized that the fruit would have to be taken out through the driveway. They would stay there and not let the truck pass through.

"I will move my rig out of the way," said Victor. Richard had immediately liked him, and asked if he could go with him. "Come on," Victor said. They had to go a quarter of a mile before they found a suitable place to park the truck. When they returned, the first load of pears was ready to leave for the packing house. The men were milling around the driveway.

"Out of my way!" yelled the truck driver. "I'm coming through!" He picked up speed, ready to take a fast, wide turn onto the pavement. The men scattered in all directions, and for a moment it seemed that he would make his escape, but a young boy drove an old Essex up to the driveway, directly in the path of the oncoming truck. The driver did not have time to stop, and the truck ran into the car, turning it on its side. Immediately the men jumped on the truck and scattered fruit in all directions. Within minutes, the three hundred boxes were demolished, pears were strewn all over the ground, and the truck itself was practically useless. From the beginning, the deputies tried to stop the men, threatening them with their guns, but when the men did not obey, the deputies did not fire, and instead attacked the rioters with nightsticks.

Richard stood to one side, holding fast to his new friend's hand. He saw Victor's father get hit on the head with a club and slump to the pavement. He put both arms around Victor's legs and tried to hold him back, but Victor shook him off and the boy fell into an irrigation ditch. When he got up, he saw Victor, a rock in his hand, looking for the man who had hit his father. And, not ten feet away, he saw him find him, and then saw him smash the man's forehead in, away from his face, with the rock.

Victor picked his father up and carried him to the side of the road, away from the melee. The old man sat up and held his head.

"Ay, what an ache of the head! What an ache of the head!" he repeated.

The fighting ended, and the two factions withdrew. Juan Rubio found his son crying under a tree and carried him to where Victor and his father sat. The young man looked at his clothes; by an unexplained miracle, he had no blood on him. A number of men had minor injuries, but the man Victor hit was still lying in the road, on the smashed pears and watermelon rinds. One of the deputies ran to the house to call an ambulance, while the others gathered around the fallen man. Almost immediately another ran after the first. "Never mind the ambulance!" he shouted. "Try to reach the sheriff instead! Joe's dead!"

"Here's the rock he was hit with," someone said. By the time the sheriff arrived, the weapon had been handled by most of the deputies.

"We questioned everybody already, Sheriff," said the deputy who had been left in charge. "No one knows who hit him, or they ain't telling."

"Let me get the son of a bitch and he'll never go to trial, I guarantee that!" said the sheriff.

"This guy is the only one who could've seen it. Says he wasn't in the fight at all. Says he was standing with the kid there, just watching."

"Come 'ere, you!" snapped the sheriff. "What's your name?"

"Victor Morales."

"What the hell you doing here if you don't belong to this here mob?"

"I stopped to see my old man. Got a load of melons I'm taking up to the City," answered Victor.

"That's right, Sheriff," said the deputy. "He give us some of them melons before the fight started. Truck's right over there."

"Okay, so you got a load of melons," said the sheriff. "Now, tell us what you know. Did you see the guy that did this to Joe?"

"No," said Victor. "I didn't see it happen. Guys were fighting all over the place, and boxes were flying off the truck. . . . Then I saw my old man get hurt, and I helped him across the road. Next thing I know, the fight's over and the guy's laying there."

The sheriff was pacing back and forth. "Goddamn it!" he shouted. "This is some mess! Joe's dead and all we've

58

got is a bloody rock and a couple of hundred sonsabitches who could've killed 'im!" He inspected the rock again, then said excitedly, "Somebody's got some blood on him. Look them all over!"

"We thought of that already. Nobody's went, and we give them all a good check," said the deputy. "No blood! Somebody musta just throwed that rock."

"How about the kid?" asked the sheriff. "You bother to question the kid?"

"I guess I forgot in all the excitement."

Richard was brought forward. "Look, sonny," said the sheriff, "did you see who hit that man? Come on, speak up!" The boy was frightened, and had difficulty phrasing his answer in English. He could not speak. "You musta seen it," continued the sheriff, "or else you wouldn't be so scared!"

The boy was finally able to talk. The sound of his voice gave him courage, and he became almost voluble. "I didn't see it. It was just like he said, everybody was running around and everything. I don't know who hit him." He looked directly into the officer's eyes to keep from turning his head to where Victor stood.

"Then why were you so afraid to talk? How come you were crying?"

"I don't talk English too good," answered Richard. "I almost answered you in Spanish."

The sheriff looked at him for a long moment, and then said, in a stern voice, "Stop lying! You know who it was! You're so scared you're shaking!"

Richard gave him a look of hurt dignity. He was not crying, now that he knew he was past the most dangerous part of this thing in which he had somehow become involved, but his voice quavered. "If you were little like me and watched a big fight and knew a man was killed, you'd be scared, too," he said as seriously as he could. He walked back to his father, and the officer did not bother him again.

"I guess the only witness was Joe," said the sheriff. "And Joe's dead." He waved his arms in a helpless gesture and, in his frustration, ordered the road cleared. He was in an uncomfortable position, he knew, for the people were

59

not itinerant laborers, but lived in town and were taxpayers. A few of them were even voters, and his treatment of them at this time could affect his re-election, but he *must* do something.

The boy who drove the car into the path of the truck was charged with reckless driving and operating a vehicle without a license, and the men were then ordered home. Only two people ever knew what really happened that morning.

The next day, the old hands went to work for Mr. Jamison and he paid them fifteen cents.

After the excitement and violence of that day, the hunger march to Sacramento was anticlimactic to Richard. He took a lunch, and there was much singing, and new country to see, but it was not more than a holiday outing to him—a happy but uneventful one. And one day Franklin D. Roosevelt was President of the United States, and another phase of Richard's life was over. The Unemployed Council was a thing of the past, and the big red barn was once more thrust into oblivion.

THREE

He had been asking her questions again, and she was a little angry. She always became quiet when he asked her things. Suddenly she sat down and pulled him onto her lap. She held his head against her breasts, and her heart was beating through her dress loudly. She talked but she would not let him move his head to see her face.

"Look, little son," she said. "Many times I do not answer you when you ask me things, and other times I simply talk about something else. Sometimes this is because you ask things that you and I should not be talking about, but most of the time it is because I am ashamed that I do not know what you ask. You see, we are simple people, your father and I. We did not have the education, because we came from the poorest class of people in México. Because I was raised by the Spanish people, I was taught to read and write. I even went to school for a time, but your father did not, and it was only because, from the time he was a small boy, he decided he would never be a peón, that he taught himself to read and write. But that is all we can do, read and write. We cannot teach you the things that you want us to teach you. And I am deeply ashamed that we are going to fail in a great responsibility—we cannot guide you, we cannot select your reading for you, we cannot even talk to you in your own language.

"No, let me finish telling you. Already I can see that books are your life. We cannot help you, and soon we will not even be able to encourage you, because you will be obliged to work. We could not afford to spare you to go to school even if there was a way for you to do it, and there is a great sadness in our hearts."

"But my father wants me to go to school. Always he tells me that, and he never takes me out of school to work, the way the other men do with their children," said Richard.

"I know. But he talks aloud to drown out the thoughts in his head and the knowledge in his heart. Inside, he knows that it is inevitable that you will have to go to work soon, for you are the only boy in the family, and when you are in the secondary school, maybe it will be the end of your education."

Her words frightened him, because she was so sure of what she was saying, and he knew that she was telling him this to save him from heartbreak at some later time; then he thought of a thing that gave him hope. "I will finish the secondary, Mamá. Of that I am sure—as long as we live in town. My father cannot take me out of school until I become of age, and I will be too young. Then, after that, things might be different and I can continue on. Anyway, the girls can help out."

"What you say is true about the secondary school, but

we cannot expect help from the girls much longer. They are growing up, and soon they will begin to marry. Their business and their responsibility will be with their husbands and their husbands' families."

"But they are young girls yet." He refused to be discouraged. "They will not possibly marry soon."

"Young? I was carrying your sister Concha when I was younger than she is now. No, my son, I know what I am telling you is true. Your father talks about you being a lawyer or a doctor when we return to México, but he knows that you will be neither and that we will never leave this place."

"But that was in México," he said. "In México, women marry young, but here we are Americans and it is different. Take the case of my teachers who are twenty-five or almost thirty years old and they have not married!"

"That is different," she explained patiently, "for they are cotorronas and will never marry. Here in your country, teachers are all cotorronas. They are not allowed to marry."

"Why?"

"I do not know. Maybe it is because parents do not want married women to have such intimate relationships with their children. I do not know."

How silly! he thought. *Mothers* are married, and what is more intimate than a child and its mother? But he did not say this to her, because his thoughts suddenly switched into English, and it occurred to him that his mother always followed rules and never asked the why of them. He had known this but had never honestly accepted it, because it seemed such a loss to him to accept the fact that his mother was not infallible. And yet in a sense she was right, for Miss Crane and Miss Broughton and two or three others were close to seventy and were still called "Miss."

Back in Spanish, he remembered what she had just said about the professions, and knew that she wanted that for him and the family more than any other thing, with the possible exception of the priesthood, and, of course, that was impossible, because he was the only son and his father would undoubtedly shoot himself if his only son became a priest. He could almost hear his father say, when she timidly sought his reaction to such a possibility, "Make nuns of all the females if that will make you happy—let the boy be, for he is on earth for other things!" And Richard smiled that he would be spared that, at least. Then he suddenly felt a responsibility so heavy as to be a physical pressure, and first he became sad that his lot was a dictate and that his parents believed so strongly in the destiny, and then he was angry that traditions could take a body and a soul—for he had a soul; of that he was certain—and mold it to fit a pattern. He spoke out then, but not in anger, saying things he sensed but did not really understand, an uncomprehending child with the strong desire to have a say in his destiny, with the willful words of a child but with the knowledge and fear that his thoughts could not possibly come true.

"Then perhaps it is just as well that I cannot go on to school," he said. "For I do not intend to be a doctor or a lawyer or anything like that. If I were to go to school only to learn to work at something, then I would not do it. I would just work in the fields or in the cannery or something like that. My father would be disappointed in me if I did get an education, so it does not matter. When the time comes, I will do what I have to do."

She was surprised at his words, and she knew then that though she could understand him better than most people, she would never really get to know him.

"But all this reading, my son," she asked. "All this studying—surely it is for something? If you could go to the university, it would be to learn how you could make more money than you would make in the fields or the cannery. So you can change our way of living somewhat, and people could see what a good son we had, and it would make us all something to respect. Then, when you married and began your family, you would have a nice home and could be assured that you would be able to afford an education for your children."

He was disappointed and tried to keep the bitterness from his voice, but could not quite succeed. "And I am supposed to educate my children so that they can change *my* way of living and they theirs, and so on? Ah, Mamá! Try to understand me. I want to learn, and that is all. I do not want to be something—I *am*. I do not care about making a lot of money and about what people think and about the family in the way you speak. I have to learn as much as I can, so that *I* can live . . . learn for *me*, for *myself*— Ah, but I cannot explain to you, and you would not understand me if I could!"

Whatever bond they had shared for a while was now gone. The magic of the moment was broken, and she talked to him once again as his superior, and her voice had that old trace of impersonal anger. "But that is wrong, Richard," she said. "That kind of thinking is wrong and unnatural—to have that kind of feeling against the family and the custom. It is as if you were speaking against the Church."

They were standing now, and she moved to the table where the masa was, and began to roll out tortillas. He tried to make her see him in his way. "Mamá, do you know what happens to me when I read? All those hours that I sit, as you sometimes say, 'ruining my eyes'? If I do ruin them, it would be worth it, for I do not need eyes where I go then. I travel, Mamá. I travel all over the world, and sometimes out of this whole universe, and I go back in time and again forward. I do not know I am here, and I do not care. I am always thinking of you and my father except when I read. Nothing is important to me then, and I even forget that I am going to die sometime. I know that I have so much to learn and so much to see that I cannot possibly have enough time to do it all, for the Mexican people are right when they say that life is only a breath. I do not know that I will find time to make a family, for the important thing is that I must learn, Mamá! Cannot you understand that?"

"I have told you I understand very little. I know only that you are blasphemous and you want to learn more in order to be more blasphemous still—if that is possible. I know that we cannot live in a dream, because everything else around us is real."

64

"But that is exactly what I mean, Mamá. Everything does not necessarily have to be real. Who said that everything has to be real, anyway?"

She was perplexed, because she had got into a discussion in spite of her ignorance, yet she was intelligent enough to find her only answer. "I do not know, but I would say God said so. Yes, God must have said so, because He says everything. When you think of Him in the way you should, you will find the answers to any question you might have."

"It is too late for that, because I cannot believe everything that He says or said." He was deeply sorry that he must hurt her. He tried to ease her feelings, but was certain that in the end he would hurt her more. "You know, Mamá, it is partly because of that that I need to learn. I believe in God, Mamá—I believe in the Father, the Son, and the Holy Ghost, but I do not believe everything I am told about Him. Last year I tried to reach Him, to talk to Him about it. I used to go out into the orchards or the meadows and concentrate and concentrate, but I never saw Him or heard His voice or that of one of His angels. And I was scared, because if He willed it so, I knew that the earth would open and it would swallow me up because I dared to demand explanations from Him. And yet I wanted so desperately to know that I found courage to do it. Then, after a long time that I did this, I stopped and tried to find Him in church, because I would be safer there; He would not destroy a churchful of people just because of me. But I never saw Him or heard Him. Then, one day, I knew that indeed He *could* destroy the church, because if He could do the best thing in the world, He could also do the most evil thing in the world. Who am I, I thought, to dare bring out that which is cruel in Him? He *is* cruel, you know, Mamá, but I believe in Him just the same. If I learn enough, I may sometime learn how to talk to Him. Some people do. You yourself have told me of miracles."

His mother looked at him as if he were not her son. She was frightened, and he thought she wanted to send him

away, but she was his mother and loved him, and therefore she conquered her fear and held him and cried, "I
have really lost you, my son! You are the light of my life
and I have already lost you," she said. In spite of himself,
his mother's tears always made him cry, and they rocked
in each other's arms. "For a moment, I thought that I
had given birth to the Devil in a little angel's body, and I
knew that I could not bear the child I carry now in my
womb. It will be born dead, I thought to myself—but only
for a moment did I think that, my son. Forgive me, little
one! Forgive me!"

His fear made him half believe that he was the Devil
incarnate. Later, when his new sister was delivered still-
born and his mother almost died, he was griefstricken
with the knowledge that he was to blame.

So now I have added murder and almost matricide to my
evilness, he thought in his heart, but his mind knew that
the tragedy had in no way been his fault. The senile mid-
wife who worked the neighborhood was as much to blame
as his mother, who obstinately refused to go to the hospital because of a certainty the doctor would be a man
and would look at her private parts.

II

It was one of those long days in Santa Clara. The sky
was a dusky blue, cloudless. The sun picked up speed as it
always does when it drops behind the mountains to the
west. Not a trace of wind was there; the trees stood perfectly motionless, as if holding their breath, hiding their
vitality within them from the world outside. The people
came out of their houses to sit on the porches, to enjoy the
cool of the evening, as they had done in their countries
miles and years away. The older boys and girls stood on
the corner under the street lamp, in full view of their
parents, laughing and exchanging banter in the free and
easy manner of happy youth. The children played in the
thickening shadows a halfblock away. The parents did not
object to their being away from the light, for they were too

young to get into trouble, and trouble had but one meaning to these people.

A boy and a girl walked slowly, hand in hand, to where the children were playing. They were timid and a little afraid, and had not wanted to come out, but their parents had sent them to play. A new game was about to begin, and a group of small children were gathered around a tree.

"Hey, here come the new kids!" said a voice. They watched with the curiosity of childhood as the new-comers approached them. One of the group moved forward. In the dim twilight, it was barely discernible that the figure was a girl. She was dressed in denim overalls and was barefooted. She had a freckled pug nose and her scraggly blond hair was gathered in back by a black ribbon. It was the only feminine thing about her.

"Whatcha want?" she asked belligerently.

"We came to play," answered the boy, in a timid voice.

"We come to play," she mimicked. "What the hell ya mean, ya come to play. How ya know we wantcha around?"

The boy was determined, in spite of his timorousness. "We want to play, too," he said.

"Watcher name?" When the boy did not immediately answer, she added, "You gotta name, ain'tcha?"

"I'm Ronnie, I'm ten. That's Mary, she's only eight."

"I di'nt astcha that, I'm ten, going on 'leven myself."

One of the boys said, "Hey, Zelda, my old lady says they're Protestants."

"No shit!" exclaimed the pugnacious girl. They all pressed around the two, critically inspecting them. There were exclamations of "Goddamn Protestants!" and "Jesus Christ!" Finally, Zelda said to the boy, "You can play, but she can't 'cause she's a girl. We're gonna 'nitiate ya."

"What do you mean?" asked Ronnie warily.

"We're gonna pants ya, stoopid!" The boy started to run, and she shouted, "Hold 'im, ya guys!" In a moment, they had him on the ground. His sister began to cry.

"Leave him alone," said Richard.

"You shut up, blackie, or I'll kick ya inna ass," said Zelda. They quickly took the pants off the kicking boy and tossed them over a fence. Across the street, some girls were jumping rope. "Manuel," said Zelda to one of the boys, "take the rope away from those kids an' we'll hang 'im."

"Aw, come on, Zelda. Leave him alone," said Richard.

"Goddammit! We'll do the same to you," she said, and started toward him. Richard ran, and barely reached his house ahead of her. "Come out! Come on out!" she screamed. Richard's mother began to scold her in Spanish. The girl turned to her. "Shut up, ya sonuvabitchen black Messican! Shut up!" Tears of impotent rage streamed down her dirty face.

Juan Rubio took his belt off and beat his son on the legs and buttocks with it. "Go out there!" he said angrily. "I'll show you what will happen to you any time you run from a girl!"

Richard went out, and Zelda bloodied his nose and split his lip. Then she ran back to the tree. Richard went into the house and cried with his mother, thankful that his father did not beat him for losing the fight.

Ronnie's father, hearing his little girl's screams, arrived on the scene. The boys cowered from the angry man. One of them retrieved the boy's trousers and threw them to him.

"Whatcha sore about?" asked Zelda. "We wuz jes' playin' wit' 'im." But she, too, kept her distance.

The boy was taken home. His mother made him a cup of hot tea and comforted him as he cried. The father kept repeating, "You should have heard her, May. She swore like a grown man. God! I think she would have *really* hung him."

"By the legs, Daddy," said Mary. "She said by the legs."

"The ruffians! Barbarians!" The mother was highly incensed. "I knew we shouldn't have come to this place. Living with this foreign element. Maybe there isn't even a church for us here!"

68

At the mention of the word "church," the boy said, "I'm going to be a minister."

"You hear that, Will? Maybe the dear child has been called," the mother said to her husband.

"Called, hell," he said. "The kid's scared to death, that's all. Thinks he can fight them that way." But he knew that the boy's future was decided; she would never let any of them forget that her son had been chosen.

"We should have stayed in Oregon with our own people," she said.

"Oh, Christ! I'm going to bed," said Will.

It was months before Ronnie and Mary were again allowed to play with the neighborhood children. They walked to and from school, hand in hand, and when they were home, they stayed indoors or played in the back yard. Once, Zelda waylaid them on the way home from school and beat Ronnie up. "Tha's jes' to show ya I can beatcha," she said. Ronnie and Mary had never seen her wear a dress, for she went to the parochial school and their school hours were different.

The months went by, and one day Mary stayed after school to get a library book. A young teacher sat behind a desk in the small room that was used as the school library. She looked up and saw Mary hesitate at the doorway.

"Come in," she said, in the pleasant voice young teachers affect. "You're Mary Madison, aren't you? Well, I'm certainly happy to see someone else in this school who wants to read. That's my only customer over there," she said, pointing to Richard, who was leafing through some books. She felt she could make Mary more at ease by bringing him into the conversation. "What shelf are you on now, Richard?" Her voice sounded false even to her.

"Why do you ask, Miss Moore? You know exactly where I am," answered Richard.

"Will you help this young lady select a book?" She turned to the girl and smiled. "Go ahead. He'll help you." Goddamn kid, she thought; he was always disconcerting her. He expected to be treated like an adult at all times.

69

Oh, well, she must get her papers graded if she was to be free tonight. She was only a short time out of normal school, but her ideals about schoolteaching had already disappeared, and she was pretty enough to have her fun whenever she desired. If these kids only knew, she thought, with a satisfied smile.

"Hello, Richard," said Mary.

"Hi, Mary."

"You don't have to help me if you don't want to. Gee, Miss Moore is so nice! Why do you have to talk so mean to her?"

"She gives me a pain. I hate dumb teachers."

Mary was horrified. "You shouldn't say things like that! You know teachers are the smartest people there are."

"Okay, if you say so," he said. He turned away from her.

"Is it true what she said? That you read all these books?"

"You said yourself that teachers don't lie."

"They don't," said Mary. It surprised him that she had not missed his sarcasm. "Why do you always want to be real mean?"

He talked to her as if he were someone very old. "I don't want to be mean. I used to think just like you do, only worse. You know, I even used to think that teachers didn't make number one or number two, like God or the saints."

"Richard!" She gasped, and her face was very red.

"Really," he continued, very seriously. "Every time I went to the basement, I used to try to imagine Miss Moore or even Miss McElhenny, who's much nicer and smarter than any old teacher they have around here, and I used to try and try to picture them doing it, but I just couldn't. I knew they wouldn't sit like that and then wipe themselves like that. And one day I saw a teacher smoking, and she tried to hide the cigarette, and I felt bad because I knew that they were just like everybody else."

Mary held her hands to her ears. "Stop it! You hear? Stop it! You're just talking dirty, and I won't listen."

"Okay," said Richard. "It isn't dirty, but if you think it is, I won't talk about it any more, but you know another reason I changed my mind about teachers?"

Mary was almost in tears. "If you can talk decently, I'll listen. Otherwise I'm never going to talk to you again."

"Well, the teachers teach us all kinds of things, and sometimes they're not really honest about it. . . . Sometimes I read things in books that show me teachers are wrong sometimes. I guess they think we're too dumb to know about two sides to a story. Like Benedict Arnold was an Englishman, to begin with, and he wasn't really a traitor—to the English people he was a kind of a hero, and things like that. All of them—the teachers and the sisters and the priest—they all lie to us sometimes. I don't know why, but they do, and it makes me feel real dumb. The Father tells us the Protestants are all going to Hell, and it's wrong for us to even go into a Protestant church, and I bet your preacher tells you we're all wrong. They can't all be right, and I don't like them to always tell me that they know everything, that's all."

"I don't know what you're talking about," said Mary, "but let's be friends, Richard. Did you really read all those books?"

"Yeah." He was disappointed that she did not sympathize with him.

"Gee, it must have taken forever and ever!"

"Nah," he said, embarrassed because he was pleased at her words. "One every night. Except on Fridays. She lets me take four or five over the weekend."

"Gosh!" She was properly impressed.

He appreciated her admiring exclamation, and felt he would like to do something for her. "If you want," he said, "I'll see if she'll let you take more than one. Today's Friday."

"All right," she said.

He reached up and handed her a book. "You'll like the *Campfires*," he said. "They're girls' books."

"You read girls' books?"

"I used to when I was little. They're not as exciting as

71

the *Swifts* or the *Rovers,* but I got to read them all." She did not ask why, and he liked her for it. "Look," he asked her suddenly, "you want to see my books? The ones I got at home, I mean."

"I guess so," she answered.

"Well, you go home. I can't walk with you, 'cause the guys might see me. Ask your old—your mother to let you come over my house."

"I don't think she'll let me," she said, disappointed by the sudden realization. "She says you're all heathens."

"What the hell's a heathen?"

"I don't know, except that it's not a nice thing to be. Mother says all Catholics are heathens."

"Jesus Christ! Your old lady must be crazy!"

"Don't say bad things about Mother, Richard. And you don't have to swear. You're not like the others."

"The hell I'm not. You just said so yourself."

"All right," she said, with finality. "If you're going to be naughty, I'll—"

"Okay, okay," he said. "Gee! Maybe you're a little bit nuts yourself. Ask her anyway, will you? And I'll be waiting for you at home, just in case. Okay?"

"All right, Richard," she said. "I'll ask her."

Richard was reading in the bedroom when his mother called him. "There is an americanita outside, son. I think she wants to see you," she said.

He ran out and brought her in by the hand. "It is the protestantita, Mamá. Her name is María, and I am going to show her my books."

"She is very skinny, this one," said his mother aloud. She cannot possibly be any good for bearing children, she thought.

Mary stood speechless with wonder as Richard and his mother spoke to each other in Spanish.

"My mother says that you are welcome and that this is your house," Richard told her.

"My house?" she asked dumbly. This was an entirely new world to her. She had a sudden urge to make her excuses and flee.

72

"She means to make yourself at home," he said, feeling suddenly sorry that she could not speak their language.

"Oh," she said, in a small voice, and changed her mind.

"Come in here," said Richard, "and I'll show you my books." He pulled a wooden box from under the bed and handed her a book. "That's my favorite," he said. "I've read it six times. It's about a boy and a monkey. You can take it home if you want."

"She talks funny," she said.

"We all do. That's the Spanish."

"Is it hard to learn?"

"I don't remember. Talking *this* way was hard to learn, though. You want to know something?"

"What?"

"A long time ago, the Spanish was the only way I could talk. Then I went to school, and they taught me to talk like this. I've been trying to teach my father and mother to talk English, but I don't think they really want to learn."

They looked through all his books, laughing over the illustrations and talking about the myriad things children talk about. Within a half hour, they were close friends. And always, even when the topic discussed was trivial, they spoke and acted almost like adults. When he had finished telling her about the books, he showed her his collection of ancient daguerreotypes, and they pondered over these reproductions of people they did not know.

"Sometimes I get sad when I look at these pictures," said the boy, "because they are so old that the people in them are sure to be dead already. Sometimes I can just stay hours thinking of who they were and what they were like, and I get mad at the people that threw the pictures away."

"Where did you get them?" asked Mary.

"Out the pit. I got most all my books there, too."

"What's the pit?"

"The city dump. People throw all kinds of things out there. If you want to go the next time I go, I'll take you." He was not afraid to be seen with her now. "If you promise not to tell anyone, I'll tell you a secret."

"All right."

"I found a Bible there once. I gotta keep it hid, so my mother doesn't find out about it."

"I should think your mother would be happy to know that you have it," she said in surprise. "Mother reads to us from the Bible every night."

"It's all right for Protestants to read it, but it's a mortal sin for us heathens. I'm going to finish it before I tell the priest, though. And, boy, will I get it then!"

It was too complicated for her, so she said nothing.

"Come out in the back," he said. "We got a funny house, but we got the best back yard around. All kinds of trees and a big barn in the back." They sat in the shade of a fig tree. "You know what?" said Richard. "I'm gonna write books when I grow up." He immediately became embarrassed. "I never told anyone that before."

She touched his arm. "Do you want to read a poem I wrote?" she asked softly.

"Okay."

She pulled a piece of paper out of her pocket and handed it to him. "I brought it just in case," she said, and kept her head lowered as he read aloud:

"Trees are nice but I like flowers,
Specially after heavy showers.
Their petals are bright and filled with dew,
All kinds of colors and smell nice, too."

He looked at her with admiration and surprise. "It's beautiful! And you're a girl, too! I can't write pretty things like that. I just write about donkeys and boys."

"Donkeys?"

"Well, everybody writes about horses or dogs. I want to write about donkeys, and say nice things about them, for a change. I save everybody at the end, though," he explained, because he did not want to seem too unconventional. "I'll show you sometime."

"All right. I'm glad you like my poem. I'll show you some more next time." She carefully folded the piece of paper and put it in her pocket. They walked around the yard, and he got her a tomato from the garden. They inspected the big barn, breathing in the pleasant staleness of it.

"I don't know why," said Richard, "but I like the smell of horseshit."

"Richard!" she exclaimed.

He was surprised. "Well, what do you call it, then?" he asked.

"Manure," she said. "You don't have to always be vulgar."

"That's something else," said Richard, "and I'm not vulgar. Manure is something you use to make things grow. I ought to know, because my father works on ranches. When you're talking about ranches, you say manure, but when you're talking about horses doing it, it's—the other."

"Mother says we should never use that word."

"You have to use it, Mary—or else how are you going to say it when you want to talk about it? They got a word to explain things like that, when it is all right to use a word and when it isn't, but I don't understand it too good yet. Something about a relative."

"I don't care," said Mary. "I'm just not going to talk about it."

They went back into the house. Richard's mother placed some thick Mexican chocolate and some tortillas with melted cheese on the table for them.

"Will you come to my house sometime?" asked Mary as they ate.

"No."

"Why not? I came here, didn't I?"

"I don't like your brother," he said. "He's a snob."

"What's a snob?"

"I don't know for sure, but there was guy like him in a book I read once, and nobody wanted him around because he was a snob."

She thought for a moment. "Maybe he seems to be funny because he's going to be a minister."

"A minister!" Richard laughed. The idea was so ridiculous to him that he said, in Spanish, "¡Ese no lo será!" Then, because Mary was staring at him, he said, "Not that one, he won't, I'll betcha!"

"He will, too! He will, too!" she almost screamed.

"No, he won't. You know why? Because preachers are like our priests and everybody likes them, and nobody's gonna like your brother, because he's a snob."

"He is not a snob!" she sobbed. "And you're being mean!"

Richard realized he had been cruel, and besides he was easily defeated by tears. "Okay, okay!" he said placatingly, trying to restore the harmony that was lost. "So I admit I'm wrong. Ronnie's a good guy, but, for Christ's sake, don't cry!"

"Stop swearing at me," she said angrily.

"All right, Mary," he said, and handed her his handkerchief. "I'm sorry." She wiped her eyes and sat silent. After a time, he asked her if she was angry with him.

"No, not any more," she answered. Then she added, in a serious voice, "But you're going to have to remember that Ronnie's my brother, and you and I are going to be best friends. You don't have to like him, but I don't want you to say bad things about him."

"I promise," he said.

"No, don't promise," she said, with the wisdom of a grown person. "Just do it because you want to be my friend."

"I'll go over your place if you want me to," he said, anxious to make amends.

"I have to go home now," she said. "Mother worries about me."

Richard walked her home. As he left her at her gate, he said, "I'm going to call you Mayrie from now on. That's the way they pronounce it in the Bible. I looked it up."

"All right, Richard," she said.

"Did you have a nice visit, dear?" her mother asked her when she walked into the house. "She visited the Mexican's home, Will," she said to her husband, for the third time.

"Yes, Mother," answered Mary. "Except just before I left, Richard said something that made me angry."

"What did he say?" asked her father.

"He told me that Ronnie was a snob."

"What a horrid thing to say!" exclaimed her mother.

The father laughed, and said, "Come now, May. The kid wasn't far wrong. You *are* making a snob out of our boy."

"Because I teach him he's better than the riffraff around here?" she asked angrily. For years, she had tried to rid her husband of his boorish ways, and was beginning to despair over the prospects of changing him. Her son, however, was going to be a little gentleman. And now that he had a vocation, her efforts would redouble to see that he had a home life worthy of the honor he would bring to it. She caught sight of the book Mary carried in her hand. "Where did you pick up that dirty thing?" she asked.

"It belongs to Richard. He loaned it to me," answered Mary.

"It's filthy," said her mother. "Take it out to the porch, and tomorrow you return it to him. The idea, handling a dirty thing like that! You might catch something from it!"

"Oh, Jesus, May!" exclaimed her husband. "Let her read it. After all, the kid was good enough to lend it to her. She can't insult him by telling him it's dirty."

She gave him a look of scathing reproach. "He was good enough to lend her a load of germs, that's what he was," she said. "And listen to me, Will. Just because you don't seem to care a bit about the welfare of the children, don't think for a minute that I'm going to shirk my responsibility, too!" She looked at him, wishing for a retort, and when it did not come, she said to Mary, "Now, do as you're told!"

The little girl was close to tears in her disappointment. "He said he was sorry the book wasn't too clean, but he said that only the words counted. He said that no matter how dirty the pages were, the words on them made them like clean. Please, Mother. May I read it?"

"Oh, all right," said her mother. She could be generous, for she had just won another victory over her husband.

"But keep it outside and read it there. I'll not have it in my clean house."

"Thank you, Mother!" exclaimed Mary happily. She suddenly felt full of strange information she must give them. "You know," she said, "they *are* different—his people—but they're very nice. Richard's mother gave me something to eat."

"You ate there?" asked her mother in alarm.

"Now, what the hell's wrong with that?" asked Will.

"It'll spoil her dinner, for one thing, and besides who knows what those people eat?" Really, how could Will be so blind to the things that could harm her children!

"It tasted good," said Mary, but decided not to go into a description of the food. "They talk funny—Spanish he called it. I'm going to learn to talk that way."

"I knew a feller once who knew the lingo," said her father. The mother went to the kitchen, and Mary climbed on her father's knee.

"Daddy."

"Yes, Sis?"

"I like him."

"That's good. You should like everybody."

"I didn't mean that, Daddy," she said. "I mean I like him for a husband. I'm going to marry him."

"Oh?" He attempted to sound serious. "Does he know it yet?"

"No, but he likes me. Then, when we're married, I'm going to make him change a little, so he'll be just right."

"You shouldn't, Sis. That wouldn't be very nice—to change him. After he changes, maybe you won't like him." Without realizing it, he had become serious.

"You know how I know he likes me? He said, 'You're the smartest Goddamn girl around!'"

"Is that a compliment?"

"Oh yes, Daddy!" She put her arms around his neck. "The best ever!" But her father was not listening to her now.

FOUR

João Pedro Manõel Alves was forty years old when he came to Santa Clara. He arrived from Point Loma, shaken and sick from a three-month tour on a fishing boat that had taken him to the Galápagos and on down the lower west coast of South America. João was not a workingman, and was accustomed to better food than the slush his fellow-countrymen fed him on board the boat, so when he was paid his share of the boat's haul, he said goodbye to the friends he had made in the few days he had spent on the beach and took a Greyhound stage north. His ticket was to San Francisco, because the agent said he had to have a ticket to somewhere, but he had no set destination in mind. He stopped off at Santa Clara, because he remembered that back in his native city of São Miguel, in the Azores, he had heard of a Portuguese settlement in that town.

Because João was not a talkative man, he found it easy to get along with the people in the beginning, and soon rented a small shack near the tannery for twenty-five dollars a year. With the little money he had left, he bought two cows and made his living from the milk he got from them. It is true he rarely had spending money, but he ate well and was happy in his solitary life. The people of Santa Clara thought him somewhat of a celebrity, because he was a newcomer and but a year away from the old country. They invited him to dine in their homes, plying him with sopas and good muscatel. Then they would sit back and wait for him to talk of the islands. They would give names of relatives and friends, in the hope of finding a mutuality that would bring him closer to them in this alien land, but João disappointed them by recognizing few names and not knowing any of the people at all. The good folk of Santa Clara knew that he was not a common one, for he spoke the language of the aristocracy, and they rejoiced, for here was a good man for the Society of Santo António or the Society of the Holy Ghost. They began to call him Dom João, and made him an honorary member of the committee in charge of the Festa do Espiritu Santo, but João made the unpardonable sin of declining the exalted position. The Holy Ghost did not interest him in the least. The truth of the matter was that he was an agnostic, but could not offend the people by telling them. So from then on they left him to himself, occasionally referring to him as "that queer one," or "that maluco João." And because the Portuguese language is so, his name was soon corrupted to João Pete. As the months went by, it changed to Joe Pete Manõel, and it was as Joe Pete Manõel that Richard first became aware of him.

Now that his reticence, which had at first made him favorable, labeled him as odd to his neighbors, his one remaining virtue in the eyes of the town was the fact that he loved children. And this virtue led directly to his misfortune. These days, Joe Pete Manõel was seen only in the afternoons, when he took his cows to graze. It would have been more convenient for him to lead them across the railroad tracks and into the field, but Joe Pete Manõel knew what pleasure the children derived from the sight of his animals, so he walked across town, feeling like a modern piper as the children followed him along the way. Some of them went with him into the fields, and played while he whittled small figures or made whistles for them out of reeds. Or they would come near the animals and run their small children's hands over the soft hide when their young minds assured them they had nothing to fear. Every few weeks, the little faces were replaced by new ones, for as the novelty ceased to exist, the fickle children would desert Joe Pete Manõel. The girls would return to their dolls or jacks, and the boys discovered that shooting robins with slingshots was more fun, and besides the birds were good eating.

Of all the children who went with him, there were two who remained loyal to him. One was a shy, retiring girl with solemn dark eyes, and the other was the boy Richard Rubio. The boy did not sit with Joe Pete Manõel from his own choice at first. He had two goats, and it was easier to take them out to graze than to bring grass to them, so he would go out and tie them to a tree, then sit on the grass and talk to the man. The girl, who was named Genevieve Freitas, had come as often as she could since the first time, when she was nine years old. She would rush home from school, do her chores hurriedly, and go out to the fields for an hour. She always sat a few feet away from the man and the boy, and always carefully arranged her dress over her brown legs. Richard never heard her speak more than two or three words at a time.

From the first, Joe Pete Manõel found the young boy a good audience for his soliloquies, and then gradually the relationship became more than that to him. He began to note that the boy was absorbing everything he said to him. Also, there was an innate communicableness in the small, honest face that made the man speak out and say things he had withheld even from himself. Their first attempts at conversation were fumbling and entirely unsatisfactory, because the man knew only a few words of English, but one day Joe Pete Manõel said:

"You spik da Portagee?"

"I can understand it if you go slow," said Richard.

"Unnastand? Goot!" said the man. "You talka da Spañol, I talka da Portagee. Hokay?" And the arrangement was satisfactory to both of them.

Another day, the man said, "The Azores, they are very similar to this."

"Do they have prunes and apricots there, too?"

"Not in large orchards, but people grow them in their gardens. There we have olive groves and vineyards. My father has a large plantation."

"You are a rich one, Joe Pete Manõel?" asked Richard.

"Rich? No, not the way you mean. My father is a rich

one—a very rich one—but, by God, I am richer in my own way."

"Tell me of your father," said the boy, not fully getting his friend's meaning. The man fixed a long gaze on him, his mind going back through his life.

"I will tell you, Richard Rubio. My father is a stapud. You know what that is?"

"I know only that it is a bad word," said Richard.

"In the English, you say it 'sombitch.' My father is that, a sombitch, but in the Azores he is a great man. Governor-General he was at one time. The people here do not know that I remember seeing some of them when I was a young boy. They worked in my father's orchards or his stables. Some of them sold fish or vegetables in the streets. In the Azores, it is not a great honor to sell fish or vegetables, as it is here in Santa Clara, and I was not allowed to talk to them, for they were below my station. Now the same people look down upon me, but it does not matter greatly."

"You are sad, Joe Pete Manõel?" asked the boy.

"Perhaps it is because I am human—perhaps I am not what I think I am, my child. Sometimes at night, when I am lonely, I find pleasure in thinking that I am better than these people. And I know how wrong I am, because no man is better than another, any more than every man is equal, simply because we are all different from each other. Every one of us has his own meaning of the word 'better' —his own meaning of any word. So I have fought that feeling all my life, even though I was always taught I was superior to those around me.

"You see, Richard, there is much more to it. My father is a blood relative of Dom Manõel, the last King of Portugal. Until the time I was almost twenty years old, my father was titled, and when, in 1910, Portugal became a republic, he gave up his title and became a politician. An opportunist he was, and I, who had been taught all my life by tutors, was sent to the continent to study law. I had had my wife selected for me when I was five years old, and was but a few weeks from marriage when I went to Lisboa. She was beautiful, and the few times I saw her and we were allowed to talk a little, we agreed how fortunate it was that we loved each other. This does not always happen when marriages are arranged. But her father would not renounce his loyalty to the aristocracy, and my family called off the wedding. 'For political reasons,' they said."

"Why did you not run away with her?" asked Richard.

"I was young and weak, and did not have the courage to go against the wishes of my father. Also, I could not support her, for I had no money. So I went to the university in Lisboa, but did not like that of being a lawyer. I spent all my time in the library, reading the classics."

"What are they?" asked Richard.

"The greatest books ever written. You cannot imagine how large the library was at the university. Soon my father received word that my work was unsatisfactory, and a suggestion that my calling was maybe for something else, but he wrote back and said they must make of me a lawyer. He was high in the favor of the government, and they had to do what he said. I wrote verses, and had some great times with literary friends, and then something happened." He stared again at the boy. "I do not think I shall tell you of that," he said.

"Please, Joe Pete Manõel, I want to hear all of it!" said Richard.

The man looked unseeingly at the tall grass for so long that the boy thought he would not speak any more that day. Suddenly he began again, "No, rapaz, I will skip that part. But the next day I arranged passage for the islands.

"What a scene my father made when I appeared in São Miguel! I was his only son, his heir. Three sisters I had, but they would soon marry and take another name. 'You have borne me four daughters, woman!' he screamed at my mother. Although he was now a republican, he secretly wished for the return of the monarchy. He had a fanatic desire to preserve his line. Now he denied me the right to enter his house, in an effort to make me do as he wished. I secured a position on the faculty of the lyceum in São Miguel. For fifteen years, I taught philosophy and lived to myself. He would not even allow me to visit my mother, so she had to visit me. Then she died, and the old one remarried, for political reasons. His wife is young but barren, and I am still his heir.

"After my mother's death, I found courage to leave my position, and went to the Madeiras. From there I went to the African colonies, but I could do nothing but teach. My mother left me a little money, and with it I paid my passage to America. In New York I was lost, so I searched for a place where I could be with some of my own kind. I was running away from my people, and yet I could not live without them, so I went to San Diego. The life of a fisherman is a difficult one, and I came here. Now I am really happier than I have ever been. For a time, I used to be frightened, because something was happening to me. I found myself strongly attracted to men. Not in the strong sexual way, and not men I knew, but just anyone I chanced to see on the street. I had suddenly, when I did not expect it, a strange urge to kiss a man walking past me. But that has disappeared now."

"On the lips, Joe Pete Manõel?"

"Yes, on the lips, but no more than that."

"That is strange enough," said Richard, "that of kissing another man, who is not your father, on the lips—but I am not sure I understand what you mean by 'more than that,' although I think I do, but I am not sure."

"Someday you will understand," said Joe Pete Manõel. "Enough time for that."

The boy was not satisfied, but intuitively he knew when he should not press the older man. He asked, "And now what will you do, Joe Pete Manõel?"

"Now? I will remain as I am. I have no great desire out of life, and am really happy enough. It is not often that I give way to depression."

"Maybe you should have a woman," said Richard. "My father says that a man should have a woman if only to do the work around the house."

"Perhaps in time, my wise little friend," said Joe Pete Manõel. Yes, he thought, before long I will surely be well again.

From that day, the two talked as often as possible, and the man began to see in the boy a reflected justification for his own misspent life. He talked to him of the many places he had seen in his travels, and spoke at length of the beauty of the outdoors and of the great arts of the world. And sometimes he would have fears for the boy, and did not speak for days. At other times, the same emotion made him rave and storm, shouting fierce and unintelligible words, until, at last, he would clasp the boy tightly in his arms and cry. And although Richard did not fully comprehend the reason for these outbursts, he was not frightened by them and did not question the man.

Once, the boy said, "I am worried, Joe Pete Manõel."

"Why, rapaz?"

"It is the Immaculate Conception. It is giving me much trouble these days. How? How?"

"Do not bother yourself with such thoughts. You are very young, and there are so many things—beautiful things —with which to employ your mind."

Richard's concern made his voice almost tearful. "You are the smartest person I know, Joe Pete Manõel. Smarter even than my teachers, and if you cannot tell me, I do not know who there is that can. Everybody I know is afraid to talk about the faith. I asked the sister in Catechism, and she looked stern, and the next time I confessed, the priest told me that there are some things we are not to ask about, but just believe. He is close to God, and I did not want to make him angry, so I did not say anything—but why do *you* always refuse to talk to me about the faith?"

Joe Pete Manõel smiled tenderly, and he sounded pleased when he spoke. "I do not talk to you about some things because I treat you like a man, boy. And a man must find out some things for himself, inside himself. You are one person, and I am another person, and I would do you great wrong to teach you what I feel, because to you it should only be important what *you* feel."

Richard understood, but his problem was far from being solved. "There are but three things that I can say I have learned for myself. First, I know that one should never discuss matters of sex with one's parents. Second, one should not, on penalty of going to Hell, discuss religion with the priests. And, last, one should not ask questions on history of the teachers, or one will be kept in after school," he said. "I do not find it in me to understand why it is this way."

His friend felt sorry for him. "All I can tell you is that you should have faith for the present, and when the time comes when you feel you do not need the belief, the doubts will help you discard it, forgetting the friend it once was to you."

"I will try to do as you say," said Richard, and he knew that his friend had told him more than he had meant to, and yet not quite enough. He was frightened, for lately he could not put doubts out of his mind very easily.

II

"One time, I was a poet," he said. It was one of those days near the end, when Joe Pete Manõel could not stop talking about life and about himself and Richard could not get his fill of listening. Suddenly he did not want to talk any more, and Richard pleaded with him to continue. Finally the man asked, "What do you know about life, child?"

Richard looked into his eyes and answered, "I learn, Joe Pete Manõel. I am learning every day."

As always, the man was very serious with him. "Do you know about women?" he asked.

"Yes."

He was quiet again for a while, and then he began to talk, although it was obvious he did not really want to do so, and he looked at Genevieve and said, "You go home now, rapazinga." He waited until she had disappeared, and then said, "I will tell you, Richard. It will not matter that you do not understand. I have tried too long to forget it, and cannot. It will do me good to speak of it.

"I was a grown man, and had not yet had a woman. Oh, I had imagined it, and had them in dreams, you know."

"I imagine sometimes, too," Richard said, interrupting him, "but I have never had such a dream." He wanted to ask him about such dreams, but he could not break into his story.

"I became acquainted with a man," continued Joe Pete Manõel. "A great poet he was, and we discoursed much. One day, he took me to his home and presented me his wife and children. A truly lovely family they made, and I was happy being with them. One time, after the children were put to bed and the serving-woman was sent home, my friend went out of the room, and immediately the woman began to kiss me. I was afraid that he would return, but she said he did not mind, and before long we were disrobed. I do not remember how it happened, but the husband was suddenly there watching us. His face was wet with perspiration and he was shaking even as I was, but not from anger. I looked up at him, but was too far in the depths of passion to think clearly about him, and went on with the lovemaking. And while I was over his wife, he did something to me. I was filled with disgust, and hated them and myself, for even *I* was now repugnant to myself. I fled the house. The act he performed I had heard about, but never in my life had I learned of a man getting pleasure from watching another man make love to his wife."

"What did he do to you?" asked Richard.

"Ah! It is too horrible to even think about it! How could *you* understand?" he said with passion. He suddenly reached out and tenderly rumpled the boy's hair, as if he felt sorry he had been rude. "Because you are young enough and as yet unspoiled enough," he said, "perhaps you *can* understand. Else why would I be telling you all this?"

But he did not tell him, and though his imagination made him weak so his knees shook, Richard knew he should not ask him again.

III

Soon it was summer. The lush fields took on their brown hue, and the blossoms, magiclike became cherries, peaches, apricots in their turn. Richard spent all the daylight hours in the orchards with his father, and did not see Joe Pete Manõel. The weeks went by, and soon it was time for him to return to school. Then, one evening, after what seemed to him like a very long time, he heard of his friend. He had come out after supper to play with the others, and someone asked him if he knew what happened to Joe Pete Manõel.

"What about him?" he asked. "Probably just Portagee gossip!"

"He gave Genevie the works!"

Something like this could not be a rumor. There must be some basis for its being said. His first thought was, Good! It was time. But immediately he realized the complications that would follow, and he was almost ill with fear for the man.

"They got 'im in jail already," said Zelda, as if anticipating Richard's question.

"They shouldn't've done that," he said.

"Why not?" asked a boy. "It's against the law for an old bastard like that to run around sticking girls!"

"The hell it was," said Zelda. "It was against a fence." Everyone but Richard roared with laughter.

"They still shouldn't've locked him up," he said doggedly.

"Boy, you sure must like 'im," said another of the boys.

"Yeah, they used to be together alla time," said Zelda. "Hey, maybe he was getting into him, too." She did not really know what she was saying, but the idea seemed to be a good one. Her followers took up her chant.

"Ah, bite me!" Richard finally said, and went home. He found his house in an uproar. His father was raging at a policeman, who was questioning him. The officer could not understand him, and one of the older girls was trying to translate.

"Tell him that he is a son of a bitch and that I should kill him for saying such a thing about my son!" roared Juan Rubio. Finally, the girl was able to convince him that the police were questioning all the neighbors, and were not making accusations. He sat down and tried to quiet his anger. The officer put his arm around the boy's shoulders and led him aside.

"Look, son. I'm gonna ask you a few questions, and you don' need to be scared a bit," he said.

"All right," answered Richard.

The officer had a notebook and pencil ready. "You know this guy they call Joe Pete Manõel?"

"Yeah."

"I hear you spent quite a bit of time with him. What did you do when you were together?"

"Talked, mostly. Sometimes we'd just sit and think, and didn't talk at all."

"You mean you jest set and didn't talk? How long did you set like this?"

"I don't know. An hour—two hours."

The officer had trouble phrasing his questions. He knew what it was he must find out, but did not know how to go about doing it. "When you talked and didn't jest set—well, what did you talk about?" he finally asked.

"Lots of things," said Richard. "He's very smart and knows about everything. He told me about the poets and painters, and all about Portugal and Africa, and about nature."

"Nature, huh?" said the officer. Now we're getting somewhere, he thought. "What about nature?"

"About the stars and planets, and about how the world really began, and many things. Did you know we're a star?"

What the hell's he mean, we're a star? Things were becoming difficult again. "Look, kid," he said firmly, "did this guy ever try anything funny with you? You know—funny?"

"You mean was he a homosexual? No, he wasn't."

This was a new word to the man. He was on the force because his sister had married a man who had something to do with the Chief of Police. It did not take unusual intelligence to be a patrolman in Santa Clara, because nothing ever happened there, except that once a year the Bank of Italy was held up. *Wise little bastard*, he thought. "Goddamn! Where'd you learn the big word?" he asked.

"I read it, then I looked it up," answered Richard. "Means *queer*."

"You say he never did anything to you?"

"No. He never touched me." He had got rid of the officer, and now he must remove the germ of doubt that was in his father's mind. His father was as fanatical about masculinity as Joe Pete Manõel was about royalty. When the policeman left, he went to his father and put his arms around him. "It is nothing, Papá. And you must not worry about me," he said in his ear. "I have the feeling for girls already." Juan Rubio held his son tightly and said, "That is the way it should be, son. That is the only way." And his voice was full of pride.

The entire town was in a state of excitement for the next few days. Over back fences women confided in low voices that they had known all along that *that* man was a bad one. *Imagine! That poor little girl, thirteen years old and with child!* By now, a dozen boys and an equal number of girls, encouraged by their parents and by the importance that was suddenly thrust upon them, "confessed" in detail to the horrible things Joe Pete Manõel had done, or attempted to do, with them. But to Richard the greatest blow was the fact that through him the prosecutor discovered that Joe Pete Manõel did not believe in God, and in the Catholic town of Santa Clara that was perhaps worse than the seduction of Genevieve Freitas.

The trial did not materialize, however, because on the third day after his arrest Joe Pete Manõel went mad. In his confusion and fright, he reverted to childhood, and reached out for the immunity he had had as a child. He called for his father, the Marquis, and told his tormentors that his greatuncle the King would hear of this abuse. It was not difficult for the authorities to commit him, and he was sent to the Agnews State Hospital for the Insane.

The girl was sent to stay with relatives in Vacaville, and a week later her family followed. Her grandmother remained in the old house, because she was too old to run away from gossip, and anyhow loose tongues did not worry her. This old woman's courage and resoluteness, which allowed her to stay in Santa Clara in the face of scandal, gave Richard one more reason never to forget Joe Pete Manõel. When the time for the girl's confinement arrived, her younger brother was sent to stay with the grandmother.

90

He was a child of six or seven, and the first time he went outside, he was immediately surrounded by Zelda's group.

"Hello, Louie," they said.

"Hi."

"How's Genevie, Louie?" asked Zelda.

The boy's parents had told him his sister was sick when they moved away, and to his young mind robustness meant good health, so he answered, "She's fine now. You should see how fat she is."

"How fat she is!" screamed the children, staggering along the sidewalk in their laughter. *"How fat she is!"*

And Richard suddenly felt sick. He would never forget that he, too, had laughed with the others. *Jesus,* he thought. *The blood of kings!*

FIVE

Juan Rubio slapped the table with his heavy hand so the dishes rattled. "Enough!" he said. "I have had my fill of your whimpering and your back talk! You are thinking yourself an American woman—well, you are not one and you should know your place. You have shelter, and you have food and clothing for you and the children. Be content! What I do outside the house is not your concern." He ate rapidly as he spoke. His face was white with anger, his lips curled back away from his gums. His mustache and cheekbones jerked up and down in unison as he chewed. His children sat around him at the table, frightened by the first harsh words they had ever heard their parents exchange.

Consuelo stood over the stove, with her back to her husband. She was frightened also, because she had dared speak to him in such a manner. This was their first argument. She trembled suddenly. In México, long ago, he had beaten her occasionally, but they had never had words. Again she shuddered. Did this mean that she would speak up more easily the next time? Somehow she knew that it was not right that she should do this—not right as it was for her friends Catalina and Mariquita, but then they were not Mexican women. Their lot was a different one from hers. She moved the rolling pin automatically, and the testal flattened and widened in perfect symmetry. It was now quiet in the kitchen, the only sound being the steady bang of the rolling pin striking the table at the start of each stroke, and the sound took hold of her and she set her face stubbornly, for this was another injustice. She wished that once, only once, she could sit to dinner with her family, but she could not. She must wait on them until they were finished, and not until then could she sit down. She knew that this was not a great thing, but it was a part of it. And the other—the cause of tonight's argument. Could he not see that it was because of her love for him that she could not stand the thought of his being with another woman?

And Juan Rubio knew that he could have set her fears at ease by merely explaining that he had not been unfaithful for years, but he could not do that, for he should not explain, should not admit, should not deny. In his mind, he would have been as right if he had done the things she had accused him of doing. He drank some water, and took his hat and coat and went out. From outside, the sound of his car came into the room as he left.

Consuelo sat down and began to cry. Her son came to her and put his arms around her, telling her she should not cry, but in the end he began to cry also. His sisters still sat at the table, weeping quietly. They had no place whatever in what had happened. Because they were daughters, they could not interfere; because they were women, they wept for themselves and their destiny—their subservience to men. They were unable to condemn their father, and they could not completely sympathize with their mother, for too well they knew that hers had been a breach of discipline, and thus etiquette.

"Has this happened before?" asked Richard of his mother.

"No. This is the first time. Even in México, when he beat me, we did not have words. He has never hit me since we came to this country, but then he knows better than to try that!" There was a smugness in her voice that he had never heard before.

"What do you mean, Mamá?" he asked.

She said, "Here in this country, the woman is looked after by the law. If your father ever put a hand on me— why, they would lock him up, that is all."

To be locked up seemed to the boy the most terrible of punishments. "You do not mean, Mamá, that you would have my father put in jail?" he asked, horrified. "Surely you cannot mean such a thing?"

Where she had been crying a moment ago, she now had a look of intense satisfaction. "I would not have to do it. There are friends that would see to it," she said.

It was inconceivable to him that there were people who would interfere with a matrimony—with the affairs of a man and his woman. Slowly his pain and sadness turned to anger. "Friends! You mean all those Spanish and Portuguese women who boss their husbands, do you not? Do you call them your friends, and is that what they are trying to do to you? Tell me, Mamá, do you want to have a husband that you can boss? Is that it?"

"We have certain rights in this country," she said. "It is not the primitive way here that it is in México. Someone told me that he was with another woman. And I do not have to stand for that any more."

"And you believed her, Mamá? You will believe anyone who comes to you with a story?"

"Why should she lie to me?" she asked as an answer, and he knew that nothing he could say would make her see it differently, but he tried.

"Mamá," he said. "Some people just like to make trouble for other people. There are bad people like that around. I do not know why, but there are. And you are a

Mexican woman, as my father said, and should not forget what you are. You have taught me that yourself. You have told me that when I marry, you want me to be the head of my family—you want me to marry a Mexican woman, because only a Mexican woman can appreciate the fact that her husband is a man. My father had women in México, and you never said a word to him about it. Why do you have to do so now?"

"You are against me, too? Is that it?" And she was ready to cry once more.

"No, Mamá," he said quickly. "It is only that I do not understand. I am not against you, and I am not against my father. It is only that I know you do a wrong thing, and I know that my father is not the kind of man that can be told what to do by anybody, least of all his woman." Once again, he was saddened by the whole thing. Sad because his mother was changing in a frightening way, and sad because it was quite possible that his father was seeing another woman. And although Richard believed that Juan Rubio had every moral right to do so, he wished that it would not be so.

"Your father will have to change his ways, Richard," she said.

"My father has already changed his ways too much. A little more would kill him."

But she did not really hear the last, because she said, "And you must help me, my son. You are with him most of the time, and you are in a position to know what he does. You must always tell me what he does."

"I will tell you, Mamá, when there is something to tell, but not for your reasons. I will tell you because I cannot bear to think of my father sneaking around to do what is his business." He had to ask her once more. "Mamá, would you really have my father put in jail?"

"Yes, I would," she said.

"I hope it never happens," he said, wishing he did not have to say it. "Because the day you do, I will leave your side forever!"

She was talking to him, but he walked away from her. There is hate in my mother, he thought. Why? Why is she changing so? Then suddenly, clearly, he saw that she, too, was locked up, and the full horror of her situation struck him. He thought of his sisters and saw their future, and, now crying, he thought of himself, and starkly, without knowledge of the words that would describe it, he saw the demands of tradition, of culture, of the social structure on an individual. Not comprehending, he was again aware of the dark, mysterious force, and was resolved that he would rise above it. It was nighttime, and black under the figtree where he lay, and he suddenly sat up and said:

"¡Mierda! ¡Es pura mierda!"

And he knew that he could never again be wholly Mexican, and furthermore he could never use the right he had as a male to tell his mother that she was wrong. Whatever differences his parents might have would affect him, but they would not concern him. It was their life, and theirs alone; he would never interfere again.

II

He was twelve that summer, and it was to remain throughout his life the one birthday that meant something to him. He did not stop to think why he was so elated that it was his birthday, but he felt a new strength surge through his sinews and loins, and he said, "I am a man," quite aloud. New clothes he had that day, and he strutted up and down the walk in front of his house, all alone, his cap set at a rakish angle, occasionally striking a boxer's pose, and cried, "Take that, and that, you lopsided, lop-eared galoot!" Then he cast a surreptitious glance over his shoulder, lest someone had seen him knocking hell out of the air. He passed Zelda's house, and his heart beat suddenly faster, for fear that she might come out and beat his cu off. Someday . . . someday—but he knew that was a lie, because he was afraid, and would always be afraid of everything. Unimportant things he was most afraid of—like being afraid of the dark and afraid of ghosts, even though he knew that ghosts did not exist, and he was afraid to fight. In short, he was a sissy, really, and he could fool a lot of people, and his mother was a lot to blame because she spoiled him, he knew, but he did not hate his mother; in fact, he loved her very much, because she was so good, really, and he loved his father, too, because he was a man and was trying to make a man of him. And the only thing he did not like his mother for was that she had placed all her love on him—had taken it away from his father to give to him, as if all the love she had left in her to give would not be enough for her golden boy, who might not be a boy, after all, because he had seen a hermaphrodite in the carnival at the Portagee fiesta, and now spent a lot of time in front of the mirror watching to see on which side he would have the breast and mustache; yet this morning when he woke up, he was twelve and a man, for he had a hardon, and it was a real good one, and did not go away until he peed.

He went inside the house to eat, and thought maybe his father would give him a dime to go see Buck Jones. He sat at the table with his chin in his hands and said aloud, in English, "I am Buck Jones and Ken Maynard and Fred Thompson, all rolled into one—I'm not Tom Mix, too, because I don't like brown horses." And he settled down to think some more.

"Of what are you always thinking?" his mother asked. "¡Por Diós! You will surely turn into a crazy with all this thinking!"

And oddly his gruff father said, "Leave the boy be! People do not think enough as it is. Leave him be!"

"Yes, Juan. But speak to him about reading so much at night. For sure he will be blind one of these days," she said.

"Blind? Bah! The boy is learning to see by reading in the poor light." And he turned to Richard and said, "Learn, my son. Learn all you can in the English, for next year by this time we will be in our country, and your knowledge will be of great benefit to you. Of course, I want you to learn our language also. What a shame it would give me if we arrived with our people and they would think I had a brute for a son."

Richard was still thinking of Silver King. "Do you think,

Papá," he said, "that when we go to México I could have a horse?"

"That is understood."

"A white one, and very big?"

"If you want," said Juan Rubio. "But why do you want a white one?"

"Because I want the best."

"Who told you that? White horses are usually little more than useless."

"You are playing with me," said Richard. "Everybody knows that a white horse is the best horse there is."

Juan Rubio laughed. "Hoo, that shows how much you know. That is only in the moving pictures, but if you knew anything about horses, you would know that a good horse is not chosen for his color."

Richard teased his father. "Mamá, does my father really know about horses?"

"That is the one thing he does know, son—that and about women," she said. "I do not think that there is anybody in the whole world who knows as much about those things as he does."

"Now, Consuelo . . ."

She ignored her husband and spoke to Richard, and he was suddenly warm with pleasure at the unmistakable pride in her voice. "Your father was the greatest horseman in our whole section of the country, and in México are found the greatest horsemen in all the world. There they have fine horses, with tiny delicate feet, which they place gently forward, one after the other—not like here, where the horses have such big hoofs."

"Those are the plow horses," said Richard. "The people who raise them make them that way—I do not know how, but they call it breeding. But the regular horses have small feet—I saw them once when the army of the infantry was camped out by the Portagee mill. They were very pretty horses, but they were all brown."

"What is this obsession about the brown?" asked Juan Rubio.

"It is only—" Richard began.

"Enough! A horse is a horse!"

97

His mother said, "I was quite a horsewoman myself—ask your father." Richard could not quite imagine his mother on a horse, try as he might. "And I did not ride the way you will see women ride here—vulgarly, astride the horse. I had a beautiful sidesaddle, which my great-grandfather made for me with his hands, but your father lost it gambling, along with the one cow we had left. Your father was never a good gambler. And what he did not lose with the cards, he managed to give away."

"But the people were very poor, Consuelo, and you did not complain."

"Oh, it is a good thing to be charitable, Juan, but"—she turned to Richard—"there were times when your father gave all our food away, and if it were not for my great-grandfather, the children and I would not eat."

"But those people perhaps did not have great-grandfathers," said Juan Rubio.

"There were times, even, when your father left the house resplendent in a new shirt and jacket, and returned only in his trousers and his hat, and for days he would walk around in huaraches, and, oh, how it hurt my heart to see your father wearing huaraches, because he was not a man of huaraches. He was a jinete—but you cannot understand what that means, to be a jinete in our country. It does not matter to have money or position if you are a jinete in our country—you are looked up to by everyone." For the first time in months, Richard recognized the tender look of longing in her face, and he knew that she had had a happiness in that remote land, in spite of the things she said of late. "And then, one day, he would come home," she went on, "wearing a new pair of boots, and it made me so happy that I could not be angry at the way he came by them."

"Did you steal them, Papá?" asked the boy.

"I do not steal, Richard," said Juan Rubio. "There are times when I find it necessary to take things, but I do not steal," and the hint of petulance that came to his mouth whenever he was purposely being absurd was there. "In this case, it probably happened that I saw a Spaniard walking alone, and his feet were just my size, so we traded footwear."

"One time," said Consuelo, "when your father came home from the war and the talk was that the Revolution was ended, we settled down and bought a store with the dowry my great-grandfather gave me. Within one month we were bankrupt, because your father gave all the food away and told the people they could pay whenever they got the money. He did not keep a record, and had no way of knowing who owed us what, even if they could pay for it. In those days, we were very lucky to still have my great-grandfather, may God have him in peace."

Richard asked, "Mamá, was your great-grandfather a rich one?"

"No, but he was independent and worked for different people, because he was not a peón."

"He was the Indian, was he not?"

"Yes, he was an Indian from the south country, but do not feel superior—you are Indian, too, as well as Spanish and probably even French."

"But my father told me I was not Spanish."

Juan Rubio was not smiling now. "We are Mexicans, Richard, that is all. Your mother has the funny idea that we carry the blood of every cuckold who has ever exploited our country, and that would include the whole world—even the gringos. She has a love for Spaniards I could never have."

Consuelo moved over to the table with the molcajete in her hand. She stood next to her husband, grinding chile as she spoke. "They were good to me. They gave me a home, and taught me all the things a woman should know, since I had no mother. Why should I not love them?"

Richard had never understood that side of his father. "But all your friends are Spanish!" he exclaimed, in a questioning tone.

"That is all there is here," said Juan Rubio, "but these people are different—they are also from the lower class, although some of them take on airs here. They are people who were stepped on, much the same as we were in our country. That is the wonder of this country of yours, my son. All the people who are pushed around in the rest of the world come here, because here they can maybe push someone else around. There is something in people, put there only to make them forget what was done to them in other times, so that they can turn around and do the same thing to other people. That is why they teach their children to call you a cholo and a dirty Mexican." It pained Richard that his father knew this. Juan Rubio noticed, and moved his hands as if apologizing for humanity. "It is not in retribution because they remember they were once mistreated, my son; it is because they forget.

"Here it is different, but in our country I was not one to associate with Spaniards, because they were the oppressors, the rich ones, and the little people struggled up from the dirt where they were trampled to lick the ass of the very people that did it to them. It still goes on. I would not associate with the priests, either, because they were on the side of the government."

"But why the priests—the men of God? They are only for the people. They do not take sides."

"Your mother loves the curates, too, but then she did not see the things I saw. On the hacienda where we were born, your mother and I, there was no Father. Twice a year, a priest from the city would come to the ranches and haciendas to hear confessions, except when the landowners needed them. Then they came every week, at a trot. When someone broke into one of the warehouses to steal some corn or beans to feed his family, the priest would arrive, hear confession, and hold Mass. Then the landowner had a fiesta for him, and he would leave. The next morning, the man who had taken the food would be found hanging from a mesquite. This sort of thing happened many times. A sane person could not hold love for those responsible for such things!"

Richard's mother was sad when she spoke. "Your father is right about that, Richard. But I was sheltered and had warmth, and it is difficult for me to feel against the men of the Church. But I must tell you that such things are true—I saw none of it, but I know it to be true and I must let you know, even though I am sick to talk against the

100

priests. Your father is a kind man, my son, and when he says the Spaniard, it does not mean that he is against the race, only that it fell upon the lot of the landowners to be Spanish!"

Richard looked at his father with a new respect. It was not like the innate respect he had for him because he was his father; rather, it was something real, for an abstract—an understanding, perhaps. He always thought, before this, that his father had first gone to join in the Revolution for a lark, to satisfy a need that his young hot blood had. Now he knew why his father had gone to fight and why, after he had married, he had left his mother to shift for herself, and had gone off again and again. Full of reverence, he looked down at the table, and the blood rose to his chest enough to stifle him, his emotion was so strong. When he looked up, he saw a flushed, nervous look on his mother's face, and noticed that his father had run his hand up under her dress, stroking the back of her knees and on up to the thighs. He looked down quickly, pleased and happy, thinking what a lovely thing it was to have his father fondle his mother, not feeling embarrassed or shocked by it. His mother moved back to the stove.

"May I have a dime, Papá, to go see Buck Jones?" he asked.

"Ask your mother."

He laughed because of his happiness and also at the childishness of his parents' little game. "You always tell me that," he said. "And if I ask her, she tells me to see you. Now that you are both here, why do you not discuss it and let me know?"

"You are perhaps to be a lawyer?" mocked his father.

"No," he answered. "I will perhaps be a soldier someday."

"No!" screamed his mother, as if he were to leave then and there. "Do not say that again, ever! You do not know about such things."

"Your mother is right," said Juan Rubio. "You cannot possibly know about such things." He stood up and put an arm around Consuelo. "He is a child and a dreamer," he explained to her softly. "The thought of the army is

101

romantically attractive to the young. I can remember that far back very easily." He reached around to the front of her dress, and she almost giggled. "Do not do that, Juan!" Her voice was low, but Richard caught the inflection. Juan Rubio laughed loudly, and gently with his heavy hand raised her braid and bit the back of her neck. She shuddered visibly, and Richard was speechless with happiness.

He forgot about the movies and went outside. Maybe things would be all right with his mother and father after all. Somehow his fears for them were removed. He skipped along for a time and then began to run. Maybe he could find the rest of the guys.

SIX

The world of Richard Rubio was becoming too much for him. He felt that time was going by him in an overly accelerated pace, because he was not aware of days but of weeks and, at times, even months. And he lived in dread that suddenly he should find himself old and ready to die before he could get from life the things it owed him. He was approaching his thirteenth year, and thought of his friend Joe Pete Manõel, though not forgotten, did not hurt as much. For the most part, he lost himself in dreams or spent hours reading everything he could find, indiscriminate in his choice through his persevering desire to learn. Now, after work, he was a familiar figure in the town library, and later, when the vacation ended, he continued the practice, for by then the meager library at school provided little for him. Yet he was disturbed by the thought that now, while he was young and strong in body, his wanderings should be physical. Imagination would do only when he became old and incapable of experiencing actual adventure.

At school, Richard was the favorite of his teachers, because his old-country manners made him most courteous in contrast to the other students. He was also a good student, and stood near the top of his class without seemingly trying. His teachers encouraged his reading, but unfortunately did not direct it, and he became increasingly complex in his moods.

It was natural that in his frantic hunger for reading he went through books he did not understand. A friend of his father had a few Spanish novels, and he read a simplified "Quixote" and made several attempts at Ibáñez, but for the first time in his life he found reading to be actual work. So he limited his Spanish reading to the newspaper he received in the mail from Los Angeles. With determination, he followed Tom Jones and Dr. Pangloss through their various complicated adventures. From *Gone with the Wind,* he emerged with tremendous respect and sympathy for the South and its people. And when the Dust Bowl families who had begun trickling into the valley arrived in increasing numbers, he was sad. They represented the South to him, and he mourned that the once proud could come to such decay.

When the boy fell asleep over a book, his father blew out the coal-oil lamp and tenderly put him to bed. Only when riding out in the country lanes was Richard forbidden to read. Twice his father threw his books out the window of the car. "Look!" he would say. "Look at the world around you, burro!" And the boy would think, What a funny one the old man is!

Indeed, the father was a paradox.

Richard went into the barn that was used to house the town's garbage wagons. Today the barn was empty of equipment and full of young guys and a few older people. Over at one end of the building stood a huge ring. It had two ropes, instead of three, and the posts were big iron pipes wrapped in burlap. There were two kids going at it pretty hard, and suddenly one of them put his hands to his mouth and stood transfixed in the center of the ring. The other one jumped around, throwing punches that either missed his opponent completely or landed on his shoulders or the top of his head. The puncher was too anxious, and the one who couldn't believe his mouth was bleeding got away, and then the bell rang.

Two other guys jumped into the ring then, and started dancing around and flexing like professionals, blowing snot all over the place, and then this local guy who was doing pretty good in the game up in the City jumped in there to do the announcing, and another guy who was already in there was the referee.

He noticed that the announcer's face was a little bumpy already, and he was already talking through his nose from fighting pro. He was a little guy and he moved around funny—real jerky, like the old silent movies—and somebody said there goes the next flyweight champ, which meant he would be the Filipino champion, since they were the only flyweights around. Richard could tell already he would not even be champ of Santa Clara, but he did not say anything, because people in small towns are funny about things like that—they think they have the best of everything.

While the two guys were fighting, Thomas Nakano came over to him. He was wearing only pants, and they were rolled up to his knees and he was barefooted.

"You gonna fight, Thomas?" asked Ricky.

"I can't find nobody who's my size and wants to fight me," Thomas said, sounding disappointed.

Richard felt his stomach begin to get funny, because he knew what was coming. "Don't look at me, Punchie," he said, trying to make a little joke out of it, but nobody laughed and it was real quiet.

"Aw, come on, Richard." He was begging him to let him hit him. "Come on, you're just my size. I'll fight anybody, only they won't let ya less'n you're the same size as the other guy."

He said no he would not, but he felt sorry for Thomas because he wanted someone to fight with him so bad. And then the guys were finished in the ring, and somebody called Thomas and asked him if he had a partner yet. He said no, but by then even guys Richard didn't know were trying to talk him into fighting him, and the pro came over, and in the end he was up in the ring shaking, because he didn't want any of these people to see him look bad. He thought back to the pictures in *Ring Magazine* and tried to imitate the poses, but before he could really decide which he liked best, Thomas was all over him. He kind of clinched and said, "What the hell you trying to do, you crazy bastard?" And Thomas said, "Don't worry— I'll take it easy," and Richard felt pretty good about then, because Thomas was his buddy and he would take it easy on him. But as they pulled away from each other, Thomas clouted him on the mouth when he wasn't looking, and Richard's head felt suddenly numb. Then Thomas was hitting him all over the place, like nobody's business—in the ribs, the stomach, and even his back sometimes, and the gloves were feeling like great big pillows on Richard's hands. It was the longest round in the history of boxing, and Thomas pissed him off. *My friend—one of the gang!* So he thought and thought, and finally, when they were apart one time, he dropped his hands and moved toward Thomas, looking real sadlike right into his eyes, as if to say, *Go ahead, kill me.* Thomas stopped also, and a funny what-the-hell's-going-on? look came to his face, and when Richard knew he was relaxed good, he brought one up from the next neighborhood and clipped him good right on the ear. Thomas spun clean around and started to walk away; then he walked in a circle and the son of a bitch was smiling, but he walked right past Richard and around the other side again, and all Richard could do was stand there and look at the crooked little legs that were browner than his. Then he heard everybody hollering for him to go after Thomas, and he thought he might as well, so he followed him around, but Thomas, wouldn't stand still. So finally he grabbed him and turned him around, and Thomas stood there grinning, and his eyes were almost closed, because his eyelids were almost together anyway. Richard couldn't hit him when he was smiling at him like that. He smiled back at him, and then the bell rang.

Richard couldn't help laughing at Thomas's grin, but suddenly he stopped, because the bell rang again and he knew he was in for it. Right away, Thomas hit him in the stomach, and Richard bent right over, and there it was— he just kept right on going, and landed on his head and took the count there curled up like a fetus. He didn't have to fight any more, and Thomas was very happy as he helped him up, and Thomas kept saying how he was like Fitzsimmons and that his Sunday punch was a right to the solar plexus. "I hit you in the solar plexus, Richard," he said over and over again, but Richard wasn't really listening to him, because he was sneaking looks at the people, and finally decided he had made it look pretty good.

The referee and the professional came over to see him. "Nice faking, kid," said the referee. "How'd ya like to be a fighter?"

"Uh-uh," he said, pulling at the laces with his teeth. The man took his gloves off.

"You don't know how to fight, but you got a punch for a kid and you're smart," he said.

"I not only can't fight, but I'm scared to fight, so you don't want me," he said.

"How old are ya, kid?"

"I'll be thirteen soon."

"I thought you was older," he said. "But, hell, I can teach ya a lot, and in a year I can put you in smokers. Make five or ten bucks a night that way."

"Not me, Mister. I don't need five or ten bucks."

"How about me?" said Thomas. "I'm the guy that won. You saw me hit him in the solar plexus." Now Richard knew why Thomas had been so anxious to fight.

"Yeah, I can use you, too," said the man, "but I want this other kid."

"Oboyoboy!" said Thomas. He had a trade now.

"How about it, kid?" asked the man. "I'm giving ya the chance of your life—it's the only way people of your nationality can get ahead."

"I'm an American," said Richard.

"All right, you know what I mean. Mexicans don't get

106

too much chance to amount to much. You wanna pick prunes the rest of your life?" Richard didn't say anything, and he said, "Look, I'll go talk it over with your old man, and I'll bet he'll agree with me. I'll bet he knows what's good for you."

"You better not do that, Mister. You don't know my old man. He's already been in jail for knifing three guys."

Richard could tell he was dumb, and, like a lot of people, believed that Mexicans and knives went together. He thought he had finished with him, but the man said, "All right, we won't tell 'im anything, and when you start bringing money home, he'll come and see *me*."

"Listen," Richard said. "He'll come and see you all right, but it won't make any difference. My old man don't feel about money the way some people do. So leave me alone, why don't you?"

But the man kept insisting, and said, "I gotta line up a smoker for the Eagles, and if you and the Jap kid here put 'em on, I'll give ya each a fin. Then, when your old man sees the dough, he'll be in the bag. What do you say?"

"Okay with me," said Thomas, "but don't call me no Jap." Richard was walking away by then, and the man followed him. "I'll give ya seven-fifty and the Jap a fin."

"No, thanks." He kept walking. They would never be able to make him do anything like that. He was sure he could be no more than a punching bag, because, hell, everybody in the neighborhood could beat him, and besides he was afraid.

The guys caught up to him, but he wasn't talking. He thought how funny the guy back there was—the fight manager. He felt that the manager was the kid and he was the grownup. *Amount to something!* Jesus! Everybody was telling him what he should make of himself these days, and they all had the same argument, except that this guy was thinking of himself. At least the little old lady who was so nice and let him read the Horatio Alger books was thinking of him when she told him he should work hard to be a gardener and someday he could work on a rich person's estate; she was sure he would be successful at that, because she had known of some Mexicans who held very fine places like that. . . . Funny about her, how the Horatio Alger books meant as much to her as the Bible meant to Protestants. . . . And the adviser in the high school, who had insisted he take automechanics or welding or some shop course, so that he could have a trade and be in a position to be a good citizen, because he was Mexican, and when he had insisted on preparing himself for college, she had smiled knowingly and said he could try those courses for a week or so, and she would make an exception and let him change his program to what she knew was better for him. She'd been eating crow ever since. What the hell makes people like that, anyway? Always worried about his being Mexican and he never even thought about it, except sometimes, when he was alone, he got kinda funnyproud about it.

As he walked toward home with the guys, he thought about the things he had just discovered. He would never really be afraid again. Like with hitting Thomas and ending the fight the way he did; funny he had never thought about that before—the alternative. Everything had another way to it, if only you looked hard enough, and he would never be ashamed again for doing something against the unwritten code of honor. Codes of honor were really stupid —it amazed him that he had just learned this—and what people thought was honorable was not important, because he was the important guy. No matter what he did and who was affected by his actions, in the end it came back to him and his feelings. He was himself, and everything else was there because he was *himself*, and it wouldn't be there if he were not himself, and then, of course, it wouldn't matter to him. He had the feeling that *being* was important, and he *was*—so he knew that he would never succumb to foolish social pressures again. And if he hurt anyone, it would be only if he had no choice, for he did not have it in him to hurt willingly.

He thought of Thomas's face in the ring, and began to laugh at the silliness of his grin, and then he laughed louder and louder, about the fight manager and all the people who tried to tell him how to live the good life, and then laughed about the guys with him, because they were laughing like crazy, too, and the sad bastards did not know what the hell they were laughing about.

II

Richard's best friend at this time was a boy with his same name but who was called Ricky. It was unusual that Richard should pick this boy as his particular friend, for he was the only person he knew to whom he could feel inferior. Ricky Malatesta first gained Richard's admiration when he fought and lost to Zelda on five successive days. At least once a week thereafter, he tried to wrest the leadership from the rugged tomboy, and was the only one in that section of town who did not fear her. Her dominance was practically the only frustration in Ricky's young life, for he could do anything. He was one of those fortunates born with the natural ability to excel at almost anything he tried, and bluffed himself through things he could not do. Whereas Richard was near the top of his class in school, Ricky *was* the top. He was an egotist of the worse species, but his personality and graceful manner gave him the virtue of modesty even when boasting. His father was a fruit-and-vegetable peddler, and Ricky seldom lacked a few cents for spending money. Richard was the only one of his acquaintances who knew him as he really was. He was aware that his friend cheated, and bluffed, and lied, but his physical prowess was in truth more than exceptional and his courage was unlimited. His intelligence was average, yet he had a talent and personality that would enable him to get anything he wanted from life, and in a way Richard admired this trait. The two enjoyed each other's company immensely, and though it is obscure what attraction Richard held for Ricky, they were inseparable.

Yet there were a great many things that Richard could not discuss with his friend. And he knew that they were slowly beginning to draw apart. He was unaware that this was because his friend was beginning to lose his glitter; that, in spite of their adolescent minds, a sense of values

109

was formulating within them, and these values contrasted so sharply that Ricky's subtlety, which generally served him so well in his relations with people, had little effect on Richard now.

"I'm gonna make a lot of money in the grocery business with my old man soon as I get out of high," Ricky said. "College is a waste of time. Someday I'm gonna have a chain of stores like the Blue and Whites, and I'm gonna get me a Aubrun or a Cord and put reflectors all over it and get a set of shave-and-a-haircut horns. Be the sharpest car around, I bet. I'm gonna be sharp, too, just watch—like my shoes. You notice my shoes yet?"

"Yeah, so you got new shoes," said Richard.

"No—I don't mean that. Look at 'em again. Them's Cuban heels. Everybody's wearing 'em."

"Oh," said Richard; then he thought, What the hell, and added, "They're sharp."

They sat on a curb waiting for a bus. Ricky stretched his legs out in front of him to admire his shoes better; then he pulled his pants leg up and said, "I'm getting hair on my legs already, how about you?"

Richard tried not to show how uncomfortable he was. "Nah, not me. Indians aren't hairy like Eyetalians."

"Yeah, I noticed you ain't got too much around your knobs yet. Let's see your leg—maybe some grew since you checked last."

"No."

"Why not?"

Richard felt embarrassment tingle along his hairline. " 'Cause my legs are dirty," he said.

"Aw, that's all right," said Ricky, and they looked but there was no hair. Richard felt affection surge through him because Ricky said nothing about his very dirty legs. They talked for a bit about the surefire methods there were for growing a mustache, and then Ricky said:

"After my old man dies, I'm gonna change my name."

Richard was suddenly depressed. "How can you talk about your father dying just like that? Don't you have any feelings or anything?"

"Sure I got feelings, and I love my dad, but everybody's

110

gotta die sooner or later and he's older'n me. I hafta work with him at first, but after the whole thing will be mine. He told me that himself. I'm going to get myself an American name, 'cause Malatesta's too Dago-sounding. I'll change it to Malloy or something."

"Jesus Christ, Ricky—Giannini didn't change *his* name!"

"No, but you noticed he changed the name of the bank." Ricky paused reflectively and then said, "I been thinking maybe I oughta get me a Jewish name, 'cause they make all the money. The bastards got all the money in the United States tied up!"

"Goddamn! Where do you get all this stuff?"

"My old man's been telling me all about it."

"You're crazy, Ricky. You think Jews are bastards because they make money, and then you say you want to make money. What does that make you? I think everybody lies about that, anyway. I bet you never even seen a Jew."

"I don't have to see 'em to know about 'em. How about you, Richard, you think you're so smart? You ever seen a Yid?"

"I see pictures of Jesus Christ all the time. He was a Jew."

"Yeah, but He was a good guy. That's why all the other Jews killed Him—anybody knows that—and besides He's God, for Christ's sake!"

"Jesus, Ricky! Here comes the bus."

"Goddamn!" said Ricky. "He's trying to run over us!" They scrambled back on the sidewalk as the bus came to a stop before them. They got to their feet and boarded the bus embarrassedly, but gave the driver a glare as they paid their fare. They sat in the rear, both trembling a little, for they had really been frightened. "Wise bastard!" said Ricky, in a loud whisper. After a bit, he asked, "How about you, Richard. What're you gonna be? You got ideas already, haven't you?"

"Yeah, I got ideas—like hitting that guy up there with a brick."

"No, I mean when you grow up—you know, what we were talking about before."

"Naw," said Richard. "I'm not gonna do nothing." And

111

as an afterthought he added, "Right now, I got the feeling I'm going to be poor all my life."

"That's okay," said Ricky. "I'll give you a job."

"Don't knock yourself out."

"Aw, Richard, I'm serious," said Ricky.

"I know you are, you crazy bastard."

They enjoyed themselves that afternoon. After the movies, they walked around San Jose, cracking wise to strange girls and making a great deal of noise in general. On the way home, Ricky blew him to an ice-cream cone.

Ricky said, "Gee, we had a lot of fun—huh, Richard?"

"Yeah. We always have fun together," he answered, and added quite naturally, "That's because we love each other."

"What the hell did you say?" asked Ricky suspiciously.

"Just that I love you, that's all," said Richard, his good mood making him unaware of his friend's fear.

"Hey, you're not going queer, are you? 'Cause if you are, I . . ."

But Richard could not hear for the roaring in his heart. Everything was spoiled now. They could be friendly, perhaps, but they could never be friends again. Then he was angrier than he had ever been. "You stupid prick!" he cried. "Oh, you stupid, dumb son of a bitch! Stupid, stupid, stupid! You had to ruin it, you're so dumb! You think you're such a smart guy, and just like that you killed one of the nicest things we both have!" He threw his cone at Ricky.

"What's the matter with you? You're the one that said—"

"Look—haven't you ever heard of having love for a friend, of loving people or things, without getting dirty about it?"

"Yeah, but two guys loving each other—that means only one thing. Maybe when you're a little kid, yeah, but I'm fourteen and you're almost as old as me."

Richard was amazed that he could not explain such a simple thing. "Jesus," he said. "You said you love your father—you thinking of sticking him or blowing him?"

"Wait a minute. . . ."

Richard was calm now, and had no desire to continue

112

the conversation. "Aw, forget it, Ricky. You're gonna be a kid all your life—just watch," he said. "I'm sorry I threw the cone at you."

"Aw, that's okay, Richard. I don't really think you're queer. You're just funnier'n hell sometimes, and then you read all that poetry and stuff."

Richard went into his house. He felt empty and suddenly very lonely. Then he thought of how, at one time, he had lived in fear lest Ricky should decide to become a writer, for if he should, Ricky would, without a doubt, be a greater one than he could ever be. And the thought that he had passed beyond Ricky made him confident once more. Confident and strangely powerful.

Richard's friends were now caught up in the erotic pastime of youth, and were, at the same time, frightened by it, as adolescents will be. They were full of fantastic theories on what would happen to them if they overindulged. The big barn in Richard's back yard became the rendezvous for the neighborhood adolescents. They clambered up into the hayloft, where they would release their desires, sometimes engaging in speed contests as an added incentive. Richard could never participate in these narcissistic orgies, because he sensed that for him there was something unnatural in the act—not morally or physically wrong but wrong in a manner he did not wholly understand. He believed that sex was too personal, too intimate, to be enjoyed in the presence of others. Yet that same intimacy demanded that a sexual experience be shared, so because masturbation was by nature a self-act, he resisted the urge.

"You don't know what you're missing," Ricky told him one day. "Why don't you do it?"

"I don't know. Maybe I'm just plain scared," he answered. "What's it feel like?"

"It's hard to explain, because it's something you feel inside. It's funny and scary, but it's so good you just keep wanting to do it over and over. Maybe it's like when you go to Heaven; you just gotta do it to find out, that's all."

And because Richard remembered reading somewhere

113

that a writer should try to live a full life in order to write about it, and because, one day, the priest would not believe him during confession, and twisted his words around so that in the end he made him admit he had done that which he had not, he finally found the courage to do it. The odor of his body as he neared the climax made him almost giddy with a pleasure that spread over all of him, until it focused in one lump in his chest, pushing, pounding, expanding, until it seemed it would choke him. And then, suddenly, a violent spasm took hold of his hips and it was over, and he could not control the shaking of his body, which now had a volition of its own.

"I'm a father! I'm a father!" he repeated crazily. He watched a part of him, the perhaps still-living glob of eggwhite-like mass, now caught in the swirling vortex of the flushed tiolet, then sucked out of sight, to eddy out to the bay.

As he sat on the toilet, trying to clear his mind and quiet his trembling body he thought, Goddamn! He's not so dumb! It *is* a little like going to Heaven.

Like the others, Richard became a slave to the practice, and now he dreaded to have to perform his bathroom functions, for although he knew about the phenomenon of reproduction, his over-imaginative mind negated his intelligence, and he had horrible visions of a dripping, deformed creature someday crawling out of the plumbing to claim him for a father in the eyes of the world. He was also haunted by fears of losing his mind, despite the fact that he had read that such a theory was a fallacy, and that you could lose your mind because of this thing only if you thought too much that it would make you crazy. It had been so easy to scoff at his friends for believing the idea, but now that he was one of them, he was not so sure as he had been. However, he was never bothered by his religion, which trained him that what he was doing was a sin. In fact, he derived great pleasure at the confessional these days, and coldly, almost objectively, he went into detail about his evil practice, because, without really understanding it, he felt that the good Padre was somehow enjoying these weekly conversations.

114

"You are insulting God," the Father would say, gently one time and with wrath the next. "He died for you, and you repay Him by continuing this hideous crime against Him. His only thought is of you, and He wants a strong mind and healthy body for you. Disease will take hold of you and kill you, my son. And you will surely go to Hell."

"Yes, Father."

"Now, this time you are really going to try, aren't you?"

"Yes, Father." But he always tried, anyway, so it made it easy to promise. Did He do it, too, when He was a kid as Jesus Christ?

"Now, how about girls, my son? Have you been doing anything with girls?"

"Only when I am playing with myself, I do it in my mind."

"Is there any one girl in particular that you think of at that time?"

"No, sometimes for a few days it can be one certain girl, and then I get tired of her and think of someone else. Different girls—a lot of movie stars, and once I tried to imagine what Sister Mary Joseph looked like if she took off all those clothes—even if she only changed to a regular dress."

The priest was horrified. "Richard, what has happened to you? How have you become so evil? You are always the politest, nicest boy—in fact, I used to think there was something almost saintly about you. You are a great disappointment to me, and, worse than that, you are a great disappointment to our Heavenly Father." His agitation was such that for the moment he forgot that the boy was not supposed to know he was recognized.

"But, Father, you must know that everyone does things like that. Don't they tell you when they confess? I know you can't tell me that, but if they don't, then a lot of people aren't making good confessions." There was no irony in his words—this matter was very serious with him now.

"We are in a confessional, my son, and here we do not

115

discuss other people," the priest said almost haughtily. "You are thoroughly evil, and that is going to rot your brain. There will be sickness and death in your family if you do not return to the path of righteousness. It is most wrong to think the things you do, and to continue with this filthy practice of masturbation. The very thought of doing such a thing is as if you had done it. The thought of the act and you are guilty of fornicating with a nun! That is a most grievous crime, and it will take you a long time to achieve redemption. I suggest you make a novena, and I am going to offer a Mass for your soul. It is done after death, usually, but I do not know of any one of the dearly departed who needs it as much as you do."

"Yes, Father." But Richard was not afraid now. It had been some time now that he ceased to be afraid of God, though he still believed in Him.

"One hundred Our Fathers and one hundred Hail Marys for penance, and now a sincere Act of Contrition." The priest bowed his head and held his hands together for a moment, then raised one up and gave his blessing almost as an afterthought.

"Oh, my God, I'm heartily sorry for having offended Thee . . ." The words came out aloud by themselves while he thought, *Ay, I'll never get out of here.*

And then the panel slid closed, and he was alone in the darkness of the cubicle and could hear a murmur from the sinner on the other side. He rose and put his palms together, crossing one thumb over the other, then with his eyes closed to narrow slits—not really closed, so he would not trip—he pushed the heavy drape with his shoulder and stepped out. He sensed the eyes of the congregation upon him. He must be a real bad one, for he had taken so long in there. The Communion was being offered, and he walked toward the altar the way he had been taught so long ago, slowly, seemingly full of reverence for the immensity of the act in which he was about to play a part—the partaking of God in the form of the Holy Ghost. Here was grace, here was absolution, if he willed it so. Then, while he still looked like one of the blessed meek, his thoughts evolved into myriad abstractions about everything but

116

what should be important right now, and when he emerged from his reverie, he was kneeling and he could see the chalice, out of the corner of his eye, three people away, then at the person alongside of him. The host was coming down between the only fingers that were allowed to touch it, and they were there in front of him, and as the paten came under his chin, he slowly stood up and backed away, staring at the paperthin white wafer, which was the Holy Ghost, still in the priest's fingers. He turned and walked along the center aisle, slowly and deliberately, until he was out on the steps. He breathed deeply, but after a moment he was very happy with his freedom. He did not know that he could never be really free.

A few days later, his father was suddenly ill. It is only a coincidence, his mind said, but in a moment of panic he repented and promised God his abstinence of everything carnal for life, if only He would make his father well. He abstained until the third day, when a faith healer came to the house and cured his father. That night, Richard did it three times to make up for what he had missed.

He never joined the others, and hid his secret from them until the day one boy said, "They say you'll grow a hair on the palm of your hand if you do it too much." In spite of himself, Richard stole a surreptitious look, and his friends howled with laughter.

Now one of the inevitabilities of life came to the fore. The boys began to look upon Zelda differently, although she still led them. She now washed her face and hair more often, and as the front of her faded overalls perceptibly filled out, she tried to behave in a more sedate manner. Not so restrained, however, as to endanger her hold on the group. Had she not felt the responsibility of her position so strongly, perhaps what happened would have been avoided, but as it was, she was forced to submit to what seemed to be predetermined.

One rainy afternoon, they were all playing in the hayloft, pushing each other and wrestling on the molding straw, when suddenly one of the boys came out of the melee bleeding at the mouth.

"You son of a bitch!" screamed Zelda. "Try coppin' another feel and I'll really hitcha!"

"Jeez, you're getting touchy," said the boy, in a whining voice. "Whatid I do?"

"Jes' keep ya han's ta yaself and shut up!"

"Hey, Zelda," said Ronnie. "How about taking off your clothes and letting us see it?"

"Jesus Christ! Listen to the preacher," said Ricky.

"Yeah, Zelda, be a sport," they all argued.

"Bull shit!" she said.

"She's chicken," said Richard.

"The hell I am!"

"You're chicken," he repeated.

In one deft motion, she was out of her overalls, and a moment later she had shed her shirt and underthings. She stood before them, her slender body rigid and her head held proudly high. The boys were speechless in their admiration. It happened suddenly, and Richard was the only one who knew she would do it.

"Your legs are dirty," he said, and she blushed. She began to gather up her clothes, and Ricky said:

"How about lettin' us, Zelda?"

"Go ta hell!"

"She's scared," said Richard. His tongue felt dry, and he had difficulty in getting the words out. He was sitting on his haunches, and Zelda walked over to him and gripped his hair tightly with both hands. She cruelly pulled his face up toward hers. "You're still scared," he said, and he was trembling.

"All right, blackie. I'm gonna do it, but after I'm gonna knock ya all over the place!" She turned to the others and said, "Okay, but not the Jap."

"They do it, too," said Richard. "How do you think he was born?"

"Yeah," said Thomas. "How ya think I got borned?"

"You don't have to let him, Zelda," said Ronnie.

"Yeah," said Ricky. "Go on, get out of here, Thomas."

Thomas did not move. "If he doesn't do it, nobody's gonna do it," said Richard.

"Who ya think you are, anyway?" said Ricky. "You

giving orders and everything around here, like you was the boss or something. Zelda's first, and I come next, and we don't want Thomas hanging around no more."

Zelda watched them with detachment. It was the first time she had not interfered in an argument. Richard said, "I just beat Zelda."

She understood and said, "All right, Thomas. After all, you're one of the gang."

"Okay, then, but I'm first," said Ricky, unbuckling his belt. "I done it before, so I know how already."

Jesus Christ! thought Richard. That Ricky!

From that day, Zelda spent very little time with the boys. It was understood now that she did not belong in the way she had, and it was only on occasions when she especially missed the old joyfulness of their camaraderie that she joined them somewhere, usually at the Rubio barn, and paid with her body for their company.

SEVEN

Juan Rubio parked his car on the road and walked across the damp yard to the house, which was built on two-foot stilts. This place never really dries up, he thought as he climbed the ladder to the front door.

"Pass, don Juan. Pass into your house," said a small dark man at the door. "What a miracle that you come to visit the poor!"

"The miracle, Cirilo, is that you find yourself at home," said Juan Rubio, with a smile. The humorous greeting was traditional, almost as if by exaggerating their state they could make their poverty bearable. "¿Cómo estás, Macedonia?" he said to Cirilo's wife.

"Muy bien, gracias a Dios, y usted, don Juan?"

It occurred to him that although these people were friends, he always spoke to them in the familiar, while they addressed him with respect. He felt a slight regret that this was so. He sat in the kitchen and thought how every time he entered a Mexican home, the woman would always be at her stove, preparing the dough or actually making tortillas. He was very conscious of this lately. Consuelo's lot was indeed a hard one. The girls must begin to do more of the work of the house. They must learn, for they would someday have their own home. He thought of his wife, and suddenly felt a tenderness for her he had never felt before, and, in fact, had not been aware of its lack. There is a Mexican movie in Mountain View tonight, he thought. I will take her with me this time.

"Pero, Cirilo," he said, "why do you insist on living here in Alviso? Soon the rains will come, and once again you will be up to your colon in mud and water."

"Ay, don Juan," said Macedonia, in mild rebuke for his indecent metaphor.

"We will leave this place," said Cirilo. "This winter we will leave this house, before Alviso once more becomes a part of the Bay of San Francisco. My old woman and I wish you and your family would come with us."

"Where are you going?" asked Juan Rubio.

"To Milpitas."

"Milpitas! But, man, that is barely two miles distant. This is not going away!"

"But it is not flood land," said Cirilo. "And there we can have our own earth. Fifty dollars for one acre, and we have saved enough living here in the sloughs so that we can purchase four acres. Since we left our country, this has been my dream—to have my own piece of ground. In México, although we knew the land belonged to the patrón, we somehow thought of it as ours, because we were allowed to grow things, and some of us kept a beast or two. In this valley everything grows. We can raise most of our food, and I can have a cow. I will have a garden and build my own house."

Now, that, thought Juan Rubio, is a good idea. To build

120

one's own house on one's own land. In Milpitas that was possible, for it was a village, but he could not do that in Santa Clara. No. The town council had a planning commissioner, even though it did not have a commission. The city engineer, they called him, could tell you what to build and what not to build. Juan thought of the thousand dollars he had earned this season contracting farm labor, and about the house on Lewis Street he could buy for twenty-two hundred dollars. But what a decision he must make! This would be good—to purchase twenty acres and borrow from the Bank of Italy with which to buy a plow horse and equipment. To get Consuelo away from foreign influences, to get his daughters far from temptation, lest one result one day with a big belly, which would mean his life, because here in America there was no such thing as a father defending the honor of his daughter.

". . . At first, we would have an outhouse, until we could afford the plumbing. It is an inconvenience, of course, now that we have been exposed to toilets that flush with a chain, but to people like us, who for so many years made caca in a corral, an outhouse should be a luxury also."

"Yes, that is so," said Juan Rubio. The reference to their life in México brought on nostalgia and regret, and a mood of slight depression. They had not been city people, he and Consuelo, but the hacienda was very like a large village, and relatives lived all around them. There had been fiestas and weddings and births and wakes. There was always activity. There had been music and laughter—here, now, there was not much laughter left. On the hacienda, people were poor but they had not been destitute. They had their house, owned by the Spaniard, but, as Cirilo had said, they thought of it as their own. More often than not, they had built it themselves. No, it would not be fair to himself and to Consuelo to take themselves out in the country to an isolated life. And, too, owning that much land would be irrevocable. It would be an admission that he would never return to México. He longed to mount a fine horse and ride into the hills, to teach his son to ride, for he was a Rubio, and a Rubio had it in him to be a horseman. He heard clearly the tingle of spurs as he walked into a house long ago, and a sudden tremor passed through his body. There was strong regret now, but the depressed mood left him. Yes, he thought, it was the *house* that allowed these people of his past, friends and relatives, to accept a lifetime of serfdom. All but himself remained on the hacienda. That he could not do, but that the house was important he knew was true. A man must have a house, place his family within it, and leave no room for authority but his own, for it was the only place a man could have authority. He wanted to return to México, and would one day do so. In another five years definitely, but for now he must reclaim his family before it was too late. He would have gone sooner, for by now it would have been time for him to settle an old score, but a religious fanatic had settled it for him not too long ago. He smiled to himself, for he thought of the man as a "fanatic," as the newspapers said, yet he knew the man had been provoked. "Long live Christ the King!" he most probably cried when he left on the mission that rid México and the world of Obregón. How different would Juan Rubio's "Viva Francisco Villa!" have been? Fanatic, yes, he had been a fanatic for he went about it like a fanatic, but only for that reason—not for killing Obregón. That ennobled the killer, but his stupidity in getting himself killed made him a fanatic.

"Have a mouthful with us, don Juan," said Cirilo's wife.

"No, thank you. I have just finished doing the same. May it do you much good."

"Do not slight us," said Cirilo.

"Well, all right, then," he answered. How odd that everything tonight should remind him! The traditional repartee before partaking of food in another's house had never seemed strange before. It was good to retain these customs, to preserve the old culture as much as possible, until his return. "I will help you build your house, Cirilo," he said. "Buy your land and we will build it in a week. There are other men who will help, and it will be like

122

building our own house. We will make our own adobe, and put one on top of the other until you have your house."

"How did you know it would be adobe?"

Juan Rubio laughed. "You do not fool me, Cirilo. You are returning to México in Milpitas."

Cirilo was serious although laughing with his friend. "That is true. I need a home, for my woman is still young and we have never been blessed with children. I see what things go on in the town. One day, she could walk off with another man, perhaps for a short hour only, but she would be used by someone else. And, too, I have a young niece who is coming from México to stay with us. It is only in my own home that I can protect them."

It is so true, thought Juan Rubio, for he had thought this very thing of his daughters, but he could not think it of his wife. There was something here. He glanced at Cirilo's wife as he ate. She was looking right at him, stared into his eyes for a moment, her face expressionless. He felt a sudden quickening in his groin. How rare! That it could happen like this. He had known her for ten years. And ten years in this country had made her forget everything she had been taught about being a wife. It happened sometimes in México that a married woman was found with a man, but not her. She was a good woman and she was devout and she was respected. But he pushed the idea out of his mind. He did not do these things any more. Yet if a woman was willing and no one knew, it did not matter if the husband was a friend.

Cirilo was saying, ". . . You, who have so many children, have a family complete. But I need a house to anchor us."

"You err," said Juan Rubio. "I also need a house. A large family can fall apart. I, too, need an anchor."

"Will you come with us, then?"

"No. I will not do that."

"But why not? You had a good season, did you not?"

"Yes, but I have decided that we are urbanites, Consuelo and I. I am going to buy a home in Santa Clara."

"You did *that* well?"

123

Juan Rubio laughed. "I was fortunate, but I could have done better," he said, "if I had not helped so many Awkies."

"They are a sad people," said Cirilo, "and they need help." He had the attitude of the poor toward the poorer.

"Precisely," said Juan Rubio. "But they were an annoyance nevertheless. I had heard of the people from Ooklahooma, but did not see one soul of them until I came home one time and there were two strange machines in the yard. More chicanos, I thought, who have lost their way, and the marshal has brought them to me, for always when Mexican people arrive looking for work, he will bring them to my house. But inside I found Consuelo making tortillas while a houseful of blonds ate ravenously. After they ate, I took them to a ranch in Evergreen, where I knew they could work cutting apricots, and then I took the men to Los Pericos, where I have standing credit for anyone I take there, and they bought a great amount of groceries. They worked three days, and on Saturday turned in their cards and were paid. They did not earn much, because they were new to the labor, but during the night they drove away somewhere." He was laughing as he told his story. "Of course, I had to pay for the groceries.

"This happened two or three times, and Consuelo would say, 'Ay, Juan Manuel. How can you be such a poor man of business—such a poor judge of people?" And I answered, 'I do not judge them. They are poorer than we are, that is all I have to know. And anyway you are the one who brings them to my attention.' 'It is the children,' she said. 'The poor little souls look so hungry.' So there you are."

"But did you not become angry? Did you not go to the police?"

"No," said Juan Rubio simply. "I could not be angry about a few dollars, which I did not need at the time. These people are not like us, I think, except for the very ancient ones of them who have had experience in being poor, and, of course, the children, who know not the reason they are hungry. They do not have the patience poverty demands, such as we have. But then, too, they have the hunger, which we do not. We have never been hungry, for we could always get beans, and beans are so good that if we were rich, we would still eat beans. And even when I was young, and was out in the brush for days and could not find game, I would encounter a young bull, make a steer of him, and make myself a meal of the balls. Have you ever eaten the glands roasted over an open fire?"

"No, no," said Cirilo quickly.

"Or rattlesnake, which is also very good. But to return to my story—that did not make me angry, that of the groceries, because they hurt no one and helped themselves, but other things they did, which made other people suffer, gave me an anger that was difficult to control. It could only happen in Santa Clara Valley, because the harvest of prunes is so unique. Some ranchers have three harvests before they are finished. Some have four, and always we must wait for the prunes to fall before we pick them, except, of course, for the last picking, when we shake the fruit off the trees. Well, you know how Mexican families come to the same rancher year after year, some for the past fifteen years. And this year the pay was two dollars a ton, and when a family from Ooklahooma arrived at a ranch and offered to harvest the crop for a dollar and a half a ton, it was easy for the rancher to tell the Mexicans who had picked his fruit for fifteen years to pack up and leave. You can see that. If the man had a crop of eighty tons, he would save forty dollars. And you can see that the Awkies, who were starving and thought there would not be enough work for everybody, would offer to work for less. But there were many Mexican families with nowhere to go, and they soon, too, were hungry, for they spend all their money coming north, and when they are through here, they spend it going to some other place. I know—I used to do it also. It perhaps is difficult for you to see that, since you have never migrated after the crops. You came to this swamp and got a job in the little cannery, and here you are. The marshal this year was at my house almost every day. 'Find work for this one,' he would say. 'Find shelter for that one.' He is a fine man. And I traveled over the valley, talking to ranchers I knew, and found a place for most of the people. Some I allowed to pitch a tent in the back yard, and it is ironic that sometimes I had Awkie families living in the yard or the barn along with Mexican families. And then the ranchers started arriving in great numbers, begging me to find a Mexican family to harvest the rest of their prunes, for the people they had hired at a dollar and a half had got their money after two pickings and left. So I helped them. I got workers for them at three dollars a ton, because the easiest and most profitable work from the point of view of the worker had been done.

"All in all, it was a busy season. Next year, this valley will get a reputation like the rest of California. It is said that the Awkie is being treated badly. Next year, they will find it difficult to work here . . . But I must go. There is a picture about Benito Juárez in Mountain View. I must go see how the films distort history."

Consuelo sat by her husband's side as they rode down the 101 from Mountain View. The film about Benito Juárez had not been very good, she thought. Somehow she resented México's heroes and México's wars. She sensed the futility of such things, for this which was to have made México really free, which was to have given the peasant liberty, had happened many years before her birth, and she could still remember the years of the Revolution. For too many years, her man had been away, perhaps to die. She remembered being evacuated from towns on trooptrains, sometimes merely because she was Juan Rubio's wife and the people who were coming to take the town were his enemies and would destroy her and her children. No, she would much rather forget about the glories of México. There was too much blood shed by Mexicans for those glories. Her son must never see any of that. The second feature, however, had been very good. A tragedy, and she had cried and cried. Everyone in the theater cried, a mark that it was a good story, and even her husband had had an itching in his eyes, for she had noticed he rubbed them. She was still a little lachrymose and sentimental. Her body felt relaxed, like after a good laxative.

She turned to her husband. From her position, his profile

was outlined against the moonlit sky. God, how handsome he is! she thought. He had always been a fine-looking man. How well he had sat a horse! How he had always carried himself with dignity! And now, as he grew older, he did not have the dash of youth, yet he seemed to grow handsomer.

"We shall go see the house on Lewis Street tomorrow, vieja," said Juan Rubio. "If you like it, we will buy it this week. What do you say to this?"

"As you might say, Juan Manuel." It did not escape her that he was discussing a big move with her. He was changing. He would not have done that a year ago—six months ago. Perhaps her conduct of late was beginning to show results. But tonight she felt deep shame for the way she had been acting, because she had been to Mexican movies and had seen Mexican wives and, for an hour or two, lived with them, so that she was wholly Mexican and knew she had been difficult. Oh, how she hoped he would do it tonight, and blushed in the dim light from the thought. They had changed so much—were changing. Thoughts like this had never occurred to her. She did not know whether it was a sin to think of these things or not, because no one had ever spoken about sex to her in her life. She had been told on her wedding day by an aunt of her husband that she should submit to anything intimate he should want to do. It would be unpleasant all her life, the aunt said, but it was the lot of all women to satisfy the desires of their man, and that was how babies were made, and God said that babies should be begotten. It had hurt that first time, hurt terribly. She was so young, had not quite fifteen years, and she thought the end of the world had come. And it had hurt the second time, a few minutes later, but as the months went by, it was no longer unpleasant, yet it was never pleasant except for the feeling of a dutiful wife. And then, after bearing twelve children, at the age of thirty-four (she remembered thinking that crazily), she felt that of which she had been unaware, and it took all her strength of will to lie still under her man, so as not to disturb his concentration, and in the darkness, with her head alongside his, she distorted her features in desire for the culmination of a mystery that drew her closer and

127

closer, and that she somehow dreaded and succeeded in avoiding. And now she could hardly wait for the next time, although she feared this new thing, and every time considered herself lucky that she was able to defeat it, and, thinking always so strongly of near climax, she did not think until too late that every stroke of the act was now a pleasure so great as to halt her breathing, that every move her husband made touched her soul. She did her chores at times not unlike a somnambulist, with a strange itchlike feeling between her legs somewhere deep inside, and now when she helped her husband bathe, she did not want to stop after scrubbing his back, but wanted to caress all the strong body with her hands, to lather his groin with soap. He did not bathe often enough. "You should take a bath more often, Juan Manuel," she would say, unaware that she was not fooling him. "The school nurse says we should bathe every day for health's sake." But he knew and would say, "For sure you are losing your mind, woman."

And then, one day, it happened so quickly that it took her by surprise and she could not resist. She gasped aloud and spoke garbled phrases, and so surprised and disconcerted her husband that for the first time in their life together he spoke to her while he himself finished the act, and in renewed passion his organ grew larger and larger, and in her contentment she tried to imitate his movements, exaggerated them so they uncoupled, a moment of great panic until they came together again, and then she tightened her arms around him in an attempt to drain everything from him in this one time.

And it was from the beauty of that initial moment of fulfillment, she knew, that she became a jealous woman.

They were home now, and she could not wait for the children to get to sleep. Her thoughts had served as an aphrodisiac to her. To her husband, she said, "Yes, it is good about the house, Juan Manuel. I would like my own house very much."

"It is better than putting money in the bank," he said as he undressed. "We will pay rent, and meanwhile we save. When we sell, I can afford to get a respectable business in our country, eh, vieja?"

128

He was unaware that he was fashioning the last link of events that would bind him to America and the American way of life.

II

Until now, Richard believed that someday they would live in México, and he fancied himself in that faraway unknown. He realized that it would be difficult for him in that strange place, for although he was a product of two cultures, he was an American and felt a deep love for his home town and its surroundings. So when he was certain the family would remain, he was both elated and sad. Glad that he would be raised in America, and sad for the loss of what to him would be a release from a life that was now dull routine.

Only through his books did he occasionally break the monotony, but the daydreams they gave rise to were no longer enough. He was a man, for all his years, he refused to accept sexual satisfaction as the sublime effort of life. There must be more to it than just that. He was aware of his need for Zelda, but did not join his friends in every orgy, because once that bodily function was taken care of, he again felt a dissatisfaction with his existence, and so, instead, he began to spend more time away from them and from home. In his wanderings, usually into the neighboring San Jose, only Ricky sometimes accompanied him. His father was still unyielding in his old-country ideas, and did not allow him to keep late hours. The same frustration that came from what he considered an unjustly restricted life, which had made him spend more time with his friends, now made him stay out later every night. The first time it happened, his father was waiting for him.

"It is late," he said. "Where have you been?"

"Walking, Papá."

"Walking? You know you are not allowed to be out after nine o'clock, do you not?"

"Yes, sir. But I must live my life," answered Richard.

"Your life! Your life belongs to us, and will belong to us even after you marry, because we gave it to you. You can never forget your responsibility to the family." He was angry now that his son questioned his authority.

"Yes, Papá, but can you not see that I cannot stand living this way?" He knew he was doing wrong by every standard his father believed in, but he could not stop talking. "Listening every day to the girls and their silly talk is as bad as listening to you and your México and to Mamá talk about God! I am sick—sick. Can you not understand?"

"Understand? What is there to understand except the fact that my son is talking back to me! Is this the American learning you are receiving? To defy your father? It is like a grown person that you sound—an errant grown person!"

"You taught me to be a grownup. From the moment I first remember, you taught me that I was a man. I was never a niño to you but a macho, a buck, and you talked to me like a man, and you took me out into the fields from the time I was five years old. Why should I not talk like a grownup? I have spent most of my life with them."

"Are you sorry I have kept you by my side wherever I go?" The hurt in Juan Rubio showed in his voice.

"No, Father. For that I am happy. I am sorry only that you will not speak to me now, that you do not try to understand me as a man, because it pleases you to think of me as a child at this moment," said Richard. "But then it has always been that way. Always you and my mother frightened me into being good. If I misbehaved, the pointer-bitch would point me out, you said, and then its paw would come forth out of the blackness and take me away. You cannot imagine what horror it was for me to think of that paw coming through walls to get me—blood still fresh on it from its last victim, who had misbehaved, too. All those ghosts, whose only purpose in our world was to help parents discipline their children—you cannot know how real they were, because you laughed and called me a child for being afraid of the dark, for being afraid even to go to the back yard and make water. . . ."

Juan Rubio reached out and ran his hand lightly across his son's cheek. His voice was soft and tremulous as he tried to control his emotion. He knew now, for the first time, that his son was no longer a child, and the realization

130

made him feel old. "That was a mistake, I see now, my son, but that is the way our people have always done," he said. "And you are right also, my son, in that you are a man, and it is good, because to a Mexican being *that* is the most important thing. If you are a man, your life is half lived; what follows does not really matter."

"But that is not enough for me, my father. I am what you say, not only because of what I carry between my legs but because I have put it to use. There must be more!"

"There is, my son. You have fulfilled but a part of your debt to your race, but you are young yet, and must fulfill the destiny of your God. When you are older, you will marry and have a family. Then you will know why you are here. That is God's will."

"No, father. That is what my mother says—I guess that is what all fathers and mothers say. We always must come back to that of the family, but if that is all there is to it, if one must marry and have a family and live like this, only working to eat and feed the family, not really living or having anything to live for, then I will never marry." His voice was pleading. "There is something inside, Father! Something I want and do not know!"

"It is God's will that we live as we do. That we raise our children and they, in turn, raise their children. Families will follow families until the end. That is how God wants it."

"Then there is something wrong with God," said Richard.

"My son," said Juan Rubio, and he was crying. "You should not say such things, for as you are I once saw myself, and as you see me you will be. I learned long ago that one cannot fight the destiny, and stopped fighting. I gave up. I know you must fight also, but in the end you will understand. I but try to save you much heartbreak."

"And you are happy, Father?"

"Yes, my son, I am happy; except when I remember. Forgive me that I cannot help you. I feel your problem, but I am not an educated one."

And Richard knew that although his father was not one of the vanquished, as he claimed, there was little resistance left. He was disappointed, and suddenly afraid, that a man who had lived such a life as his father could call this existence happiness. And he cried in his fear of this thing—this horrible, inexplicable, merciless intangible—that held humanity in its power; that made such men as his father go out every morning before sunup to harvest tomatoes, spinach, peas, or fruit, with fingers stiff from the early-morning frost and bodies tortured by the midday heat, to return after dark and eat and, too tired to love, sleep. And in the winter months they wallowed in the mud, digging out dead trees with mattocks and axes, or pruned; and, if unable to find jobs, they stood in line to claim a grocery order they had received from the State Relief Administration after having stood in another line, while all the while it rained. And they regained a portion of their longlost selfrespect, and were proud because they were feeding their families and their children would grow and raise their families.

This was happiness!

EIGHT

As the months went by, Richard was quieter, sadder, and, at times, even morose. He was aware that the family was undergoing a strange metamorphosis. The heretofore gradual assimilation of this new culture was becoming more pronounced. Along with a new prosperity, the Rubio family was taking on the mores of the middle class, and he did not like it. It saddened him to see the Mexican tradition begin to disappear. And because human nature is such, he, too, succumbed, and unconsciously became an active leader in the change.

132

"Silence!" roared Juan Rubio. "We will not speak the dog language in my house!" They were at the supper table.

"But this is America, Father," said Richard. "If we live in this country, we must live like Americans."

"And next you will tell me that those are not tortillas you are eating but bread, and those are not beans but *hahm an' ecks.*"

"No, but I mean that you must remember that we are not in México. In México—"

"*Hahm an' ecks,*" his father interrupted. "You know, when I was in Los Angeles for the first time, before your mother found me, all I could say in the English was *hahm an' ecks,* and I ate all my meals in a restaurant. Remember! What makes you think I have to remember that I am not in México? Why . . ."

"You were in the restaurant, Papá."

"Yes, well. . . . Every morning, when the woman came for my order, I would say *hahm an' ecks,* at noon *hahm an' ecks,* at night *hahm an' ecks.* I tell you I was tired, and then, one day, she did not ask, and brought me some soup and some meat. I do not know whether she felt sorry for me or whether they ran out of eggs, but I certainly was happy for the change."

"You are laughing at us," said Richard. "You yourself told me there are many Mexican restaurants in Los Angeles."

"Well, I was living in Hollywood at the time, working as an extra in the cowboy movies. There were no Mexicans to speak of in Hollywood." And he would smile in spite of himself, and the children would laugh.

"My teacher says we are all Americans," said one of the girls, who was in the first grade. She stood and began to recite, in a monotone, "I pledge allegiance to the flag—"

"You! Sit down!" said the father, in a loud voice, and laughed. "You are an American with that black face? Just because your name is Rubio does not mean you are really blond."

"It does not matter," said the little girl. "She told us we are all Americans, and she knows. After all, she is a teacher."

But all such scenes did not end with laughter, for Richard's mother was a different person altogether now, and constantly interfered when her husband was in the act of disciplining a child, and these interferences grew until they flared into violent quarrels. And Richard did not like himself, because he knew that many times he caused the disruption of family peace by playing one parent against the other in order to have his way. His mother now took to gossiping and to believing her neighbors, and Juan Rubio, who long ago had decided that he wanted nothing more out of life than to watch his children grow, saw this last vestige of happiness slipping from his grasp, and once more began to have women. Richard knew of it and was ashamed, but did not blame his father, and no longer blamed his mother, because everything was so wrong, and he was to blame as much as anyone else, and no one could do a thing about it.

So he watched the strong man who was his father; watched the raucous, infectious laugh disappear, so that he seldom saw the beautiful teeth again; watched the hair as it turned prematurely white, and the body as it lost its solidness and became flabby. Although he loved his mother, Richard realized that a family could not survive when the woman desired to command, and he knew that his mother was like a starving child who had become gluttonous when confronted with food. She had lived so long in the tradition of her country that she could not help herself now, and abused the privilege of equality afforded the women of her new country. She was not gay now; there was no gayness in her belief that her son was her world, and she proclaimed aloud that she lived only for her boy. For her, there were no songs left.

One day, Juan Rubio cooked his own breakfast, and soon after he moved into another room. Now there was no semblance of discipline whatever, and even the smallest child screamed at either parent, and came and went as she pleased. The house was unkempt and the father complained, but Consuelo, who had always been proud of her talents for housekeeping, now took the dirty house as a symbol of her emancipation, and it was to remain that way until her death.

That day, Richard saw clearly what he had helped create, and sought to repair the damage, but it was too late. What was done was beyond repair. To be just, no one could be blamed, for the transition from the culture of the old world to that of the new should never have been attempted in one generation.

II

Had Juan Rubio been faced with the problem of explaining to himself what had caused the imminent disintegration of his family, he would have been unable to do it. He was not a man to blame outside causes for his misfortunes. To him, life was to be lived, and if in its course things went badly—why, that was life, and he must act to make it as good a life as possible. He believed in God, and vaguely he believed in Heaven, but could not relate the attainment of Heaven to his actions on earth. Immortality was guaranteed under his belief in God, and, as for temporal life, it was enough that he maintain his dignity as a man, that he be true to himself, that he satisfy his body of its needs—and his body needed more than tortillas.

It was in this way, then, after having bought a home for his family and after seeing that his household was breaking up in actuality and that it was not merely a possibility, that he called for the first time at the house of adobe he had helped build in Milpitas. It was midmorning on a sunny day when he knocked on the door, and Macedonia, the wife of his friend Cirilo, opened the door and looked at him impassively.

"I wondered how long it would take you to come," she said, and he noted the resignation in her voice. But this will change, he thought. She cannot remain with this attitude after today. "How long will he be gone?" he asked, making the cuckold-to-be as impersonal as possible, for the mention of his name might be enough to make her change her mind at this delicate point in their relationship.

"Long enough," she said. He followed her into another room.

Thus it was done, and for him there could be no going back. He had returned to former custom, and he would never be weak again, nor would he compromise another time.

III

Richard walked down the street toward his old neighborhood. Though his new home was but a few blocks away, he seldom went near the old place, but on this afternoon he wanted to see Zelda, and he could not approach her anywhere else. He was excited with anticipation, and so engrossed in the pleasant thought of the girl's body that he was startled to hear his name called. He looked up to find that he was in front of the Madison home.

"Come in, Richard," said Mary. "I have something to tell you."

He opened the gate and walked up to the porch. Although they had spent many hours talking together, this was the first time he had been in her yard in the four years of their friendship. He sat on the steps and took a piece of candy she offered him.

"Fudge," she said. "I made it." After a pause, she added, "We're going away to Chicago. Daddy got a job there and we're leaving this week to meet him."

"Well, at least you get to travel," he said lightly, but was surprised to find that the thought of her leaving was saddening. She had been a good friend to him, and the only one of his acquaintances with whom he could talk about some of the things that interested him, now that Joe Pete Manõel was gone. This despite the fact that she was a girl and was younger than he.

She looked at him. "You know what, Richard? I wish Daddy would come back here. I don't want to leave."

"Why? Silly! You'll see a lot of new places and meet a lot of people. I wouldn't give up a chance like that for anything." This is true, he thought. I am a little jealous of her.

"I wasn't going to tell you until we grew up, but

136

since I'm going away, I'll tell you now." She was very frank and unembarrassed in her seriousness. "I'm going to marry you, Richard."

"Holy Christ!" he exclaimed in surprise. "Just like that, huh?" He snapped his fingers.

"No, not just like that. I knew it a long time ago, the first time I went to your house. Don't laugh at me, Richard, and please don't swear."

"I'm sorry. I forgot," he apologized. He had trained himself never to swear in her presence. He felt years older than she but he knew her moods and the intense way she had of treating anything in which she believed. He also knew her temper and the strange effect her outbursts of anger had on him. So he spoke in an older-brother tone of voice, yet was careful not to offend her, by appearing to be patronizing. "You read too many romances, Mayrie. And anyway you were sore at me the first time I took you to my house, remember?"

"You didn't take me that first time. I went. You were ashamed to be seen with me."

"You're only a little girl."

"I'm not little. I'm twelve, and you're not fifteen yet, so that makes it just right."

Her mind was really made up, so he teased her. "But what if you're ugly when you grow up?"

"That won't matter. I'm still the smartest Goddamn girl around."

"Hey, wait a minute," he said laughingly. "Now who's swearing?"

"I'm only saying what you told me," she said.

"You remember everything, don't you? It's a good thing you're going away, 'cause if you weren't, I don't know how I'd get you out of my hair."

"You never will," she said, and her self-assurance made her voice matter-of-fact. "I'll write to you, and you're going to answer. When it's time, I'll tell you to come for me." Her words startled Richard so that he felt they were both thirty years old.

"Okay, Mayrie. I'll write to you," he said, and he found he was beginning to believe her words.

"You remember that first book you loaned me, Richard? The one about the circus?"

"Yeah?"

"I cried when the monkey was shot," she said.

"That's all right," he said. "I cried every time I read it, too." He stood up. "I've got to go now, Mayrie. I'll be waiting for your letter, and I won't forget." He was already beginning to feel the loss her departure would be. "I'm going to miss you, Mayrie."

"It won't be too long, Richard." She looked down at her feet. "You can kiss me goodbye if you want to."

He leaned down and pressed his lips to hers, and wondered why he did not feel like a Goddamn fool. Jesus, he thought, a little kid like that! He turned once, but she was gone, and he walked slowly, a warmth rising in his chest making him feel a pleasure of just living. What had occurred was really a beautiful thing. Then, he walked rapidly, not looking back any more, though he wanted to do so, until he reached a group of boys playing stickinthemud on the corner.

"Hi," he said. "Zelda around?"

"Nah," said Ricky. "She don't come out much in the afternoons any more."

"What's the matter, you hard up?" asked Ronnie.

Richard looked at him contemptuously. "Why don't you shut up?" he said.

"You can see her tonight if you wanna," said Thomas. "She'll be out to play after supper."

"I guess I'll be around," said Richard. "Well, I'll see you guys after."

"Stick around," said Ricky. "You can eat at my place, so you don't have to go all the way home and back."

"Okay," Richard said, "but your old lady is gonna spaghetti me to death. Jesus, doesn't she ever cook anything else?"

"Sometimes," answered Ricky, then added, with a straight face, "We'll probably have snails tonight."

"I wouldn't doubt it," said Thomas, "you wops'll eat anything." They all laughed at the Japanese boy's remark.

"We're going to Chicago," said Ronnie proudly.

"I hope you freeze your ass off," said Richard. He suddenly realized how very much he disliked Mary's brother. "You know, I'm sorry to see Mary go, but I'm sure glad you're finally getting the hell out of here."

"What do you mean, you're sorry Mary's leaving?" demanded Ronnie.

"She's a good little kid, and I like her," said Richard.

"Listen, if you been fooling around with my sister, I'll—"

"Don't be stupid," said Richard. "She's not like you. She's got twice the brains you got."

"Just keep away from her," said Ronnie belligerently. "I'm glad we're moving away, 'cause I was getting tired of you sucking around her all the time. Calling her Mayrie, and all that. Mother never liked it, either, you know."

"Your old lady's full of what makes green grass grow, just like you are!" said Richard cruelly.

"You can't talk about my mother like that," screamed Ronnie. "Take it back! Take it back!"

"Balls!"

"Take it back, now—or I'll kick the hell out of you!"

"Oh, yeah?"

"Yeah!"

"Yeah!"

"Yeah!"

"You guys gonna yeah all day?" asked Thomas.

"Lay off, Ronnie," said Ricky. Since Zelda's fall, he was the boss.

Ronnie did not want trouble with Ricky, but he said doggedly, "Tell him to take it back!"

"Aw, shut up!" said Ricky. "Come on, Richard. Let's go eat those snails." The two boys moved off, and Ronnie said:

"My mother's right about this lousy town. No decent people at all—just a bunch of Mexicans and Japs and I don't know what kind of crud!"

Thomas hit him on the mouth, and Ronnie sat down and began to cry. They left him there.

Thomas said, "Let's go uptown, you guys, and I'll blow ya to a milkshake." They laughed at him. "Hones'. I got money. I fought a guy in Watsonville last night." They turned around and went in the opposite direction. Thomas could never be angry very long.

"Hey, Richard, how come you always picking on Ronnie? What you got against him, huh, anyhow?"

"I just can't go the sucker! You know how I hate to fight, but if he wasn't Mary's brother, I would have taken him a long time ago."

"Aw, he's all right. Just got the bighead, that's all," said Ricky. "Hey," he asked as an afterthought, "you ain't been fooling around that little kid, have you? Honest?"

"That's San Quentin quail," said Thomas, attempting to sound like a man of the world.

"Who, Mary?" Richard laughed. "Hell, no." Then, for no apparent reason, he said, "She wants to marry me." He squirmed uneasily.

"That would really fix Ronnie's water, wouldn't it?" Ricky said, laughing. Ricky could be real good sometimes.

They had their milkshake, and then returned to Ricky's house, where his father let them have a glass of Dago-red. They walked along feeling very warm inside.

"Let's go out to Bracher's orchard," said Richard.

"Jeez," said Ricky. "One thing I don't like about you is you always want to walk someplace. I musta walked about a hundred miles with you already. It wouldn't be so bad if you at least talked to me, but once you get me out in those caboulders, you don't say a word."

"You're coming, too, aren't you, Thomas?"

"Not me. I live in a berry patch, remember? I'll wait here for you guys."

"Aw, come on," said Ricky. "Maybe we can cop some cherries."

It was nighttime by the time they returned from their walk, and a game of hideandgoseek was in progress. They had long ago outgrown such games, but there seemed nothing else to do, and Zelda was playing. As they ran to hide, Richard followed her. She chose as her hiding place an indentation in the earth about two feet deep, which had been made by the removal of an old oak stump. The grass was tall, and it was dark in the empty lot.

"Get the hell away from here," she said. "This is my place!"

"I'm hiding here, too," he said.

"I'm warnin' ya," said Zelda. "Beat it!"

When he tried to get down into the hole with her, they began to fight. For fully five minutes, they struggled in the darkness. Suddenly she began to cry. It was the first time he had heard her cry when she was not in a rage. And he understood the reason for her tears. It was the end of an era for her; her dominance was over, and her life would be a different one from now on. One of her eyes was badly bruised, and her mouth was bleeding.

"Ya hurt my tit," she said, and held her left breast.

"Let me rub it," he said. "You might get cancer."

"What's that?"

"It's a sickness. If you get it, they'll hafta cut it off."

"Jesus!" she said, and was frightened. He opened her shirt and stroked her breast. She stared at him wide-eyed. Then he was tasting the blood in her mouth, and as they sank down together, he could hear the boy who was "it" chanting, "Five, ten, fifteen, twenty . . ."

When it was over, she said, "That was different, Richard."

"I know." He was lying on his back, staring at the sky. She rolled over, so that the upper part of her body was on his chest, and gently ran both hands across his forehead and down over his hair. She was enchanted that she could get such pleasure from doing that. She kissed him lightly. "You're the first guy I ever kissed," she said. Then, "I guess I love ya, Richard."

Jeez, he thought. Twice on the same day! He felt extremely good. "You're my girl now," he said. "You're going to have to be different from now on. No more overhauls, and you're going to hafta stop laying pipe with all the guys."

"Yes, Richard." She was full of happiness in her new role, and for the first time in her young life she was glad to be a woman.

141

"And you hafta quit all that swearing and fighting."

"Yes, Richard." They were quiet for a moment. Then she asked, "Why'd ya do it, Richard?"

"Why'd I do what?"

"Why'd ya make me do it with all the guys that day?"

"I don't know," he said. "I didn't care about them, but I wanted it, and that was the only way I could get it."

She thought back for a while. "I guess I musta felt this way about ya for a long time, and didn't know it even, 'cause when you told me my legs was dirty that day, I wanted to say something mean, but instead I was ashamed. I'm sorry I called ya all those names, Richard."

"That's all right. Names never hurt me."

"And I know you probably don't like to talk about it—about the guys an' up in the haylof' an' all that. I just wantcha ta know that I never did it when you weren't around. I don't know why, I just never did."

"That's not what Ricky and Ronnie say."

"I don't care, they're big liars." She was quietly angry for a moment, and then afraid that her past conduct would alienate him. "You believe me, don'tcha, Richard? You gotta believe me, because I can't be your girl if you don't."

"Sure I believe you," he said. Somehow it mattered very much to him that he should believe her, and he never thought he could be like that. "They're just jealous," he said, and he knew that in a way they really were.

Zelda kept her face averted, her head on his chest now, and was holding him tight. She knew instinctively that every possible complication must be brought out. She asked, "Richard, do you like Mary?"

"Whaddaya mean?"

She was embarrassed. "Well, everybody knows that you're with her a lot."

"She's just one of my best friends, that's all. They're moving away this week."

"I'm glad," she said. "I'm afraid of her."

He laughed but was pleased by her jealousy. "You'll never have to be afraid of Mary," he said.

The new, more drastic change that came over Zelda

was a mystery to the neighborhood. As her speech and manner improved, she became aware that she was more than a little attractive. She worked at being feminine with as much fervor as she had resisted it for so long. Her blond hair, which had not become darker, as usually happens, she had inherited from her Nordic mother, and her Portuguese father had contributed the early maturity, which, combined with years of strenuous exercise, made her at fourteen more a beautiful young woman than a pretty girl. And as she was in high school now, she made new friends and had a large following of boys. They praised her beauty, and she was pleased in spite of her self-consciousness. Because she became friendly to everyone and was accustomed to meeting boys on their own ground, she had trouble, for these new acquaintances did not know what she was like, and misinterpreted her good nature. When confronted by an overenthusiastic pursuer, she reverted to her old defense. She had yet to learn the little artifices girls use to keep insistent boys at bay yet friendly. So she resorted to her fists for protection, and when she violently spurned their advances, the boys thought of her as a teaser, and this troubled her, because she considered that the worst thing a woman could be.

Her relationship with Richard ripened into a deep love on her part and an indifferent one on his. It was understood between them that they would someday marry, and although he never told her he loved her, she was satisfied with the knowledge that she was his girl. She responded to his newfound and now everpresent dominance, and made token resistance to his whims only because it pleased him that she occasionally showed spirit. Yet she knew that she would have obeyed his every wish without a whimper. Her only fear was of pregnancy, because she knew he would leave her if that happened; he would never consent to a marriage when the reason was anything other than the desire to be with a woman for life. She loved his sensitivity and the gentleness he showed her, for she had never had such attention or encouraged it, but she was aware that he was capable of great cruelty. Only her closeness to him enabled her to see that part of his character, and

143

she was the first to recognize it. Richard himself was not yet objective enough to discover this fault in his makeup.

He visited her home when her parents and brothers were out, and sometimes they walked out of town in the evenings. The Catholic cemetery became a favorite place for their nocturnal trysts, but they were much happier when he could borrow a car and they drove far enough away so they weren't afraid of being caught. He would spread a blanket on the ground, and they would lie for hours under the stars. Their naked bodies in the wan light contrasted sharply; her whiteness paled and his brownness became swarthier. Their minds, at times like this, were free of the worry of detection, and thus, at their ease, their play and lovemaking was a thing of infinite beauty to both of them.

Few people knew that Zelda was his girl, because Richard seldom took her to movies or to dances. Nor did they spend all their time together, as most young people going steady will do. She, for the most part, stayed home, learning the many things of housewifery she had neglected all her life. She did not have girl friends, because she had never associated with girls and now found their talk silly and boring, so she strove instead to become interested in the things Richard liked. She thought reading was laborious and painful, put persevered and found enjoyment. She worked painstakingly on her schoolwork, because he scolded her about her grades and she did not want him to feel ashamed of her. And though she always knew when he became interested in another girl, she never questioned him, because in her heart she was sure of him, and they always managed to be together at least three times a week. They never tired of each other's young virility.

In this new routine, Richard lost part of the restlessness that had tortured him for so long. He still felt the need for that unknown; that substantiality that had eluded men from the beginning of time, but it lost its importance for the present. He was young, and the time for the pursuit of the esoteric would come soon enough. When the day came that he married Zelda, he would be forced to find himself, for Richard was certain that he could never revolve his whole life around marriage. He could not give that institution the importance it had falsely taken on through the centuries. Marriage, per se, was not life, nor could it govern life.

In this he believed.

NINE

Richard Rubio, lost in thought, walked slowly into his front yard. He was relaxed, although his body was bruised and sore from football practice. They had scrimmaged that day, for there was a game on Friday, and although there was little chance that he, as a scrub, would get into the game at all, he played as much during practice as the first string did. It was with the reserves that the regulars conditioned themselves and perfected their timing. Richard had almost quit when he realized that he would never make the first team, but upon reflection he knew that he enjoyed the contact and that the practice sessions took up a great deal of his time, of which there was too much for him at the moment.

The Rubio front yard was a large one, and Juan Rubio had planted a vegetable garden. There were tomatoes there now, and chiles. The driveway and the back yard, where there was another garden, were neat and orderly. At the extreme end of the property was a chicken coop, newly whitewashed, and rabbit hutches.

He reached the end of the driveway and stepped onto the porch. Then he noticed that his sister Luz sat in a car in front of the house, talking to a boy from school whom he vaguely knew. Inside the house, he was suddenly filled with sorrow mingled with disgust, as he always was these days when he came home. Trash and garbage were on the floor; bedrooms were unkempt, with beds unmade. On the floor of the living room, where two of the girls slept, blankets and a mat still lay, reeking strongly of urine, because the girls still wet their beds at the ages of eight and ten. Only his bed was made up, because his mother could not neglect him. His clothes were pressed and in order in his closet, but elsewhere he saw a slip here, a brassière there; odds and ends of clothing lay wherever the wearer decided to undress. In the kitchen, the sink was full of dishes, dirty water nearly overflowing onto the littered floor. The stove was caked with grease, its burners barely allowing enough gas to permit a flame to live.

He threw his books on his bed, then went to his mother and kissed her. She sat with one of his younger sisters between her legs, going through her hair with a fine comb. A louse cracked loudly between her thumbnails.

"Go!" he said to the little girl. "Go and bring my sisters here—and Luz, too."

"But her head smells of coal oil," protested his mother. "She cannot go out among her neighbors smelling like that."

He was angry and impatient, and his voice was harsh. "Do you think that because our house is so filthy, we are the only ones in Santa Clara who have lice?" He turned to his little sister again and said, "Go!" She jumped to her feet and ran out the door.

The girls came into the house one by one. There was a frightened look in their faces, and they immediately began to clean the house. They knew what he wanted, for this was not the first time this had happened.

"Where is Luz?" he demanded.

"She won't come in," said one of the girls. "She said to tell you to go to hell."

He walked to the car very quickly, in a rage he had never known himself capable of feeling. He said calmly, however, and in Spanish, "Go inside and help your sisters, big lazy."

"Don't bother me," she answered.

146

"What does he want?" asked the boy, from behind the wheel.

"He don't want me to be out here with you," she lied.

"Go take a shit," said the boy to Richard.

Richard opened the door and pulled her out onto the sidewalk. He slapped her hard twice, and she ran into the house screaming. The boy got out of his car, and he was big, powerful. Richard backed away toward the yard next door and took a brick from an abandoned incinerator.

"Come on, you big son of a bitch," he said. "Come after me and I'll kill you!" The boy hesitated, then moved forward again. "That's it," said Richard, "come on and get your Goddamn head busted wide open."

The boy went back to his car. "You're crazy!" he shouted. "Crazier'n hell!"

That night, for the first time in months, they had dinner together in the old way. After dinner, his father sat on the rocker in the living room, listening to the Mexican station from Piedras Negras on short wave. When the kitchen was picked up, the girls sat around restlessly in the living room, and Richard knew they wanted to listen to something else, so he said to his father, "Let us go into the kitchen. I have a new novel in the Spanish I will read to you."

In the kitchen, around the table, his mother also sat down, and said, "It is a long time, little son, that you do not read to us."

How blind she must be, he thought. Aloud he said, "It is called 'Crime and Punishment,' and it is about the Rusos in another time." He read rapidly and they listened attentively, interrupting him only now and then with a surprised "Oh!" or "That is so true!" After two hours, he could not read fast enough for himself, and he wished that he could read all night to them, because it was a certainty that he would not get another opportunity to read to them like this. They would never get to know the book, and he knew they were to miss something great. He knew also that they would never be this close together again. How he knew

147

this he could not even guess, and that was sad in itself, besides their having to do without the book.

"There are new Mexican people in town, Papá," he said. "In school today, there were two boys and a girl."

"Yes, I know," said Juan Rubio. "Every year, more and more of us decide to remain here in the valley."

"They are funny," said Luz, who, along with two or three of the girls, had come into the kitchen.

"They dress strangely," said Richard.

"In San Jose," said Juan Rubio, "on Saturday night during the summer, I have seen these youngsters in clown costumes. It is the fashion of Los Angeles."

"They are different from us," said Luz. "Even in their features they are different from us."

"They come from a different part of México, that is all," said Consuelo, who knew of such things, for she herself was different from all of them, except for her son, and this because her great-grandfather had come from Yucatán.

"Well, at any rate, they are a coarse people," said Luz. Richard and his father exchanged looks and laughed. She flushed in anger, and said in English to Richard, "Well, they ain't got nuthin' and they don't even talk good English."

He laughed louder, and his father laughed even though he did not know what she had said.

It was not until the following year that Richard knew that his town was changing as much as his family was. It was 1940 in Santa Clara, and, among other things, the Conscription Act had done its part in bringing about a change. It was not unusual now to see soldiers walking downtown or to see someone of the town in uniform. He was aware that people liked soldiers now, and could still remember the old days, when a detachment of cavalry camped outside the town for a few days or a unit of field artillery stayed at the university, and the worst thing one's sister could do was associate with a soldier. Soldiers were common, were drunkards, thieves, and rapers of girls, or something, to the people of Santa Clara, and the only uniforms with prestige in the town had been those of the CCC boys or of the American Legion during the Fourth of July celebration and the Easter-egg hunt. But now everybody loved a soldier, and he wondered how this had come about.

There were the soldiers, and there were also the Mexicans in ever-increasing numbers. The Mexican people Richard had known until now were those he saw only during the summer, and they were migrant families who seldom remained in Santa Clara longer than a month or two. The orbit of his existence was limited to the town, and actually to his immediate neighborhood, thereby preventing his association with the Mexican family which lived on the other side of town, across the tracks. In his wanderings into San Jose, he began to see more of what he called "the race." Many of the migrant workers who came up from southern California in the late spring and early summer now settled down in the valley. They bought two hundred pounds of flour and a hundred pounds of beans, and if they weathered the first winter, which was the most difficult, because the rains stopped agricultural workers from earning a living, they were settled for good.

As the Mexican population increased, Richard began to attend their dances and fiestas, and, in general, sought their company as much as possible, for these people were a strange lot to him. He was obsessed with a hunger to learn about them and from them. They had a burning contempt for people of different ancestry, whom they called Americans, and a marked hauteur toward México and toward their parents for their old-country ways. The former feeling came from a sense of inferiority that is a prominent characteristic in any Mexican reared in southern California; and the latter was an inexplicable compensation for that feeling. They needed to feel superior to something, which is a natural thing. The result was that they attempted to segregate themselves from both their cultures, and became truly a lost race. In their frantic desire to become different, they adopted a new mode of dress, a new manner, and even a new language. They used a polyglot speech made up of English and Spanish syllables,

149

words, and sounds. This they incorporated into phrases and words that were unintelligible to anyone but themselves. Their Spanish became limited and their English more so. Their dress was unique to the point of being ludicrous. The black motif was predominant. The tight-fitting cuffs on trouserlegs that billowed at the knees made Richard think of some longforgotten pasha in the faraway past, and the fingertip coat and highly lustrous shoes gave the wearer, when walking, the appearance of a strutting cock. Their hair was long and swept up to meet in the back, forming a ducktail. They spent hours training it to remain that way.

The girls were characterized by the extreme shortness of their skirts, which stopped well above the knees. Their jackets, too, were fingertip in length, coming to within an inch of the skirt hem. Their hair reached below the shoulder in the back, and it was usually worn piled in front to form a huge pompadour.

The pachuco was born in El Paso, had gone west to Los Angeles, and was now moving north. To society, these zootsuiters were a menace, and the name alone classified them as undesirables, but Richard learned that there was much more to it than a mere group with a name. That in spite of their behavior, which was sensational at times and violent at others, they were simply a portion of a confused humanity, employing their self-segregation as a means of expression. And because theirs was a spontaneous, and not a planned, retaliation, he saw it as a vicissitude of society, obvious only because of its nature and comparative suddenness.

From the leggy, short-skirted girls, he learned that their mores were no different from those of what he considered good girls. What was under the scant covering was as inaccessible as it would be under the more conventional dress. He felt, in fact, that these girls were more difficult to reach. And from the boys he learned that their bitterness and hostile attitude toward "whites" was not merely a lark. They had learned hate through actual experience, with everything the word implied. They had not been as lucky as he, and showed the scars to prove it. And, later on, Richard saw in retrospect that what happened to him

150

in the city jail in San Jose was due more to the character of a handful of men than to the wide, almost organized attitude of a society, for just as the zootsuiters were blamed en masse for the actions of a few, they, in turn, blamed the other side for the very same reason.

As happens in most such groups, there were misunderstandings and disagreements over trivia. Pachucos fought among themselves, for the most part, and they fought hard. It was not unusual that a quarrel born on the streets or backalleys of a Los Angeles slum was settled in the Santa Clara Valley. Richard understood them and partly sympathized, but their way of life was not entirely justified in his mind, for he felt that they were somehow reneging on life; this was the easiest thing for them to do. They, like his father, were defeated—only more so, because they really never started to live. They, too, were but making a show of resistance.

Of the new friends Richard made, those who were native to San Jose were relegated to become casual acquaintances, for they were as Americanized as he, and did not interest him. The newcomers became the object of his explorations. He was avidly hungry to learn the ways of these people. It was not easy for him to approach them at first, because his clothes labeled him as an outsider, and, too, he had trouble understanding their speech. He must not ask questions, for fear of offending them; his deductions as to their character and makeup must come from close association. He was careful not to be patronizing or in any way act superior. And, most important, they must never suspect what he was doing. The most difficult moments for him were when he was doing the talking, for he was conscious that his Spanish was better than theirs. He learned enough of their vernacular to get along; he did not learn more, because he was always in a hurry about knowledge. Soon he counted a few boys as friends, but had a much harder time of it with the girls, because they considered him a traitor to his "race." Before he knew it, he found that he almost never spoke to them in English, and no longer defended the "whites," but, rather, spoke disparagingly of them whenever possible. He also bought a suit to wear when in their company, not with such an extreme cut as those they wore, but removed enough from the conservative so he would not be considered a square. And he found himself a girl, who refused to dance the faster pieces with him, because he still jittered in the American manner. So they danced only to soft music while they kissed in the dimmed light, and that was the extent of their lovemaking. Or he stood behind her at the bar, with his arms around her as she sipped a Nehi, and felt strange because she was a Mexican and everyone around them was also Mexican, and felt stranger still from the knowledge that he felt strange. When the dance was over, he took her to where her parents were sitting and said goodnight to the entire family.

Whenever his new friends saw him in the company of his school acquaintances, they were courteously polite, but they later chastised him for fraternizing with what they called the enemy. Then Richard had misgivings, because he knew that his desire to become one of them was not a sincere one in that respect, yet upon reflection he realized that in truth he enjoyed their company and valued their friendship, and his sense of guilt was gone. He went along with everything they did, being careful only to keep away from serious trouble with no loss of prestige. Twice he entered the dreamworld induced by marihuana, and after the effect of the drug was expended, he was surprised to discover that he did not crave it, and was glad, for he could not afford a kick like that. As it was, life was too short for him to be able to do the many things he knew he still must do. The youths understood that he did not want it, and never pressed him.

Now the time came to withdraw a little. He thought it would be a painful thing, but they liked him, and their friendliness made everything natural. He, in his gratefulness, loved them for it.

I can be a part of everything, he thought, because I am the only one capable of controlling my destiny. . . . Never—no, never—will I allow myself to become a part of a group—to become classified, to lose my individuality. . . . I will not become a follower, nor will I allow myself to become a leader, because I must be myself and accept for myself only that which I value, and not what is being valued by everyone else these days . . . like a Goddamn suit of clothes they're wearing this season or Cuban heels . . . a style in ethics. What shall we do to liven up the season this year of Our Lord 1940, you from the North, and you from the South, and you from the East, and you from the West? Be original, and for Chrissake speak up! Shall we make it a vogue to sacrifice virgins—but, no, that's been done. . . . What do you think of matricide or motherrape? No? Well—wish we could deal with more personal things, such as prolonging the gestation period in the Homo sapiens; that would keep the married men hopping, no?

He thought this and other things, because the young are like that, and for them nothing is impossible; no, nothing is impossible, and this truism gives impetus to the impulse to laugh at abstract bonds. This night he thought this, and could laugh at the simplicity with which he could render powerless obstacles in his search for life, he had returned to the Mexican dancehall for the first time in weeks, and the dance was fast coming to a close. The orchestra had blared out a jazzedup version of "Home, Sweet Home" and was going through it again at a much slower tempo, giving the couples on the dancefloor one last chance for the sensual embraces that would have to last them a week. Richard was dancing with his girl, leading with his leg and holding her slight body close against his, when one of his friends tapped him on the shoulder.

"We need some help," he said. "Will you meet us by the door after the dance?" The question was more of a command, and the speaker did not wait for an answer. The dance was over, and Richard kissed the girl goodbye and joined the group that was gathering conspicuously as the people poured out through the only exit.

"What goes?" he asked.

"We're going to get some guys tonight," answered the youth who had spoken to him earlier. He was twenty years old and was called the Rooster.

The Mexican people have an affinity for incongruous

153

nicknames. In this group, there was Tuerto, who was not blind; Cacarizo, who was not pockmarked; Zurdo, who was not left-handed; and a drab little fellow who was called Slick. Only Chango was appropriately named. There was indeed something anthropoidal about him.

The Rooster said, "They beat hell out of my brother last night, because he was jiving with one of their girls. I just got the word that they'll be around tonight if we want trouble."

"Man," said Chango, "we want a mess of trouble."

"Know who they are?" asked the Tuerto.

"Yeah. It was those bastards from Ontario," said the Rooster. "We had trouble with them before."

"Where they going to be?" asked Richard.

"That's what makes it good. Man, it's going to be real good," said the Rooster. "In the Orchard. No cops, no nothing. Only us."

"And the mud," said the Tuerto. The Orchard was a twelve-acre cherry grove in the new industrial district on the north side of the city.

"It'll be just as muddy for them," said the Rooster. "Let's go!"

They walked out and hurriedly got into the car. There were eight of them in Zurdo's sedan, and another three were to follow in a coupé. Richard sat in the back on Slick's lap. He was silent, afraid that they might discover the growing terror inside him. The Rooster took objects out of a gunnysack.

"Here, man, this is for you. Don't lose it," he said. It was a doubledup bicycle chain, one end bound tightly with leather thongs to form a grip.

Richard held it in his hands and, for an unaccountable reason, said, "Thank you." Goddamn! he thought. What the hell did I get into? He wished they would get to their destination quickly, before his fear turned to panic. He had no idea who it was they were going to meet. Would there be three or thirty against them? He looked at the bludgeon in his hand and thought, Christ! Somebody could get killed!

The Tuerto passed a pint of whiskey back to them. Richard drank thirstily, then passed the bottle on.

"You want some, Chango?" asked the Rooster.

"That stuff's not for me, man. I stick to yesca," he answered. Four jerky rasps came from him as he inhaled, reluctant to allow the least bit of smoke to escape him, receiving the full force of the drug in a hurry. He offered the cigarette, but they all refused it. Then he carefully put it out, and placed the butt in a small matchbox.

It seemed to Richard that they had been riding for hours when finally they arrived at the Orchard. They backed the car under the trees, leaving the motor idling because they might have to leave in a hurry. The rest of the gang did not arrive; the Rooster said, "Those sons of bitches aren't coming!"

"Let's wait a few minutes," said the Tuerto. "Maybe they'll show up."

"No, they won't come," said the Rooster, in a calm voice now. He unzipped his pants legs and rolled them up to the knees. "Goddamn mud," he said, almost good-naturedly. "Come on!" They followed him into the Orchard. When they were approximately in the center of the tract, they stopped. "Here they come," whispered the Rooster.

Richard could not hear a thing. He was more afraid, but had stopped shaking. In spite of his fear, his mind was alert. He strained every sense, in order not to miss any part of this experience. He wanted to retain everything that was about to happen. He was surprised at the way the Rooster had taken command from the moment they left the dancehall. Richard had never thought of any one of the boys being considered a leader, and now they were all following the Rooster, and Richard fell naturally in line. The guy's like ice, he thought. Like a Goddamn piece of ice!

Suddenly forms took shape in the darkness before him.

And just as suddenly he was in the kaleidoscopic swirl of the fight. He felt blows on his face and body, as if from a distance, and he flayed viciously with the chain. There was a deadly quietness to the struggle. He was conscious that some of the fallen were moaning, and a voice screamed, "The son of a bitch broke my arm!" And that

155

was all he heard for a while, because he was lying on the ground with his face in the mud.

They halfdragged, halfcarried him to the car. It had bogged down in the mud, and they put him in the back while they tried to make it move. They could see head-lights behind them, beyond the trees.

"We have to get the hell out of here," said the Rooster. "They got help. Push! Push!" Richard opened the door and fell out of the car. He got up and stumbled crazily in the darkness. He was grabbed and violently thrown in again. They could hear the sound of a large group com-ing toward them from the Orchard.

"Let's cut out!" shouted the Tuerto. "Leave it here!"

"No!" said the Rooster. "They'll tear it apart!" The car slithered onto the sidewalk and the wheels finally got traction. In a moment, they were moving down the street.

Richard held his hands to his head. "Jesus!" he ex-claimed. "The cabrón threw me with the shithouse."

"It was a bat," said the Rooster.

"What?"

"He hit you with a Goddamn baseball bat!"

They took Richard home, and the Rooster helped him to his door. "Better rub some lard on your head," he told him.

"All right. Say, you were right, Rooster. Those other cats didn't show at all."

"You have to expect at least a couple of guys to chicken out on a deal like this," said the Rooster. "You did real good, man. I knew you'd do good."

Richard looked at his friend thoughtfully for a moment. In the dim light, his dark hair, Medusalike, curled from his collar in back almost to his eyebrows. He wondered what errant knight from Castile had traveled four thou-sand miles to mate with a daughter of Cuahtémoc to pro-duce this strain. "How did you know?" he asked.

"Because I could tell it meant so much to you," said the Rooster.

"When I saw them coming, it looked like there were a hundred of them."

"There were only about fifteen. You're okay, Richard. Any time you want something, just let me know."

Richard felt humble in his gratification. He understood the friendship that was being offered. "I'll tell you, Rooster," he said. "I've never been afraid as much as I was tonight." He thought, If he knows this, perhaps he won't feel the sense of obligation.

"Hell, that's no news. We all were."

"Did we beat them?" asked Richard.

"Yeah, we beat them," answered the Rooster. "We beat them real good!"

And that, for Richard Rubio, was the finest moment of a most happy night.

II

And yet oddly, despite the chances he took, it was while in the company of his childhood friends that Richard became involved with the police. It happened so suddenly that he had no chance to prepare himself for the experience.

Ricky had a car now, and the gang was going to get him skirts for it as a sort of a present. They searched all over San Jose until they found a car with a set that would look good on Ricky's, but they had not even started to take them off when two night watchmen, on their way home from work somewhere, stopped them. The men really had nothing to hold them on, because they nad not done anything yet, but Richard knew they did not need a reason.

The guards had them lined up against the firehouse when the squadcars arrived. The lead car had not yet come to a complete stop when the rear door opened and the first cop jumped out. He kept moving toward then in one motion, and as Richard was the closest to him, he got it first, in the face, and the back of his head hit the brick wall and he slid down to the sidewalk. The guys jumped the cop then, crying and swinging, but it was a futile attack, because the rest of the officers were out of the cars by then, and they simply beat them to pieces. They were thrown into the back of the cars bodily, and were lucky they did not hit the side of the car as they went through the door. They were hit and jabbed in the ribs all the way to the city jail. The cars went down a ramp into the cellar of the joint, and they were pushed and dragged into a large room. First all their belongings were taken from then and put in individual paper bags, and then a big man in plain clothes came in.

Richard asked where he could lodge a complaint against the officers for beating them, but the detective just grinned.

"Resisting arrest," someone said.

The plainclothesman went into the buddybuddy act with them, and laughed as if the whole thing were a great joke.

"What were you going to do to the car, fellows?" he asked almost jovially.

They did not answer him. One of the cops went over to Ricky and hit him under the ear, and, when he fell, gave him the boots.

"Goddamn pachucos!" he said.

"Now," said the detective, "maybe one of you other guys wants to tell me."

They remained silent, and were all given another beating. Richard's head ached, and he was frightened. He remembered that when he was a kid, a friend of the family had been picked up for drunkenness, and was later found dead in his cell under mysterious circumstances. He realized he must say something—anything.

"We weren't doing anything," he said. "Just fooling around town when those guards hollered at us, and we stopped to see what they wanted."

"How about the girls? Had any idea in mind about the girls?"

"What girls?"

"The two girls walking by—don't make out you don't know what I'm talking about. You Goddamn bastards think you can come here and just take a clean white girl and do what you want! Where you from, anyway? Flats? Boyle Heights?" He really thought they were from Los Angeles.

"We're from Santa Clara and we don't run around

raping girls." The detective slapped him with the back of his hand. He looked at him for a minute and said:

"Don't give me that crap. You little bastards give us more trouble than all the criminals in the state. . . . God, I wish we had a free hand to clean out our town of scum like you! Now, you're going to tell me! What were you doing by that car?"

Richard decided to keep silent, like the others, and the detective left the room. Then a cop began taking them one by one. Ricky was halfcarried into the other room, and Richard began to think about how rough it all was. Strange how the police thought they were zootsuiters. Hell, they all had on Levis and wore their hair short.

Ricky was brought back almost immediately, and Richard could see by the stubborn expression on his face that he had not said a word. He could also see that he was frightened, too, but still game as hell. They took one of the others in, but he also came out almost immediately, and the cop motioned to Richard. He knew then that the detective would not waste time with the others, because while they had been silent, he had at least answered some of the questions. But he did not really know what to expect.

"Sit down, kid." The detective's approach was different this time. "Tell me all about it." Richard almost laughed, because now he was being conned; and he suddenly realized that this was the last of it and the detective would not hold them, because he had nothing to keep them on.

"There isn't anything to tell," he said, and the officer made a little joke about how Richard was the only one who would speak up, and how that showed he was not afraid, like the others—though he knew all along it was just the opposite. And Richard knew that he knew this, but now he was over his fear and talked to him calmly, not with the voice he had earlier, when he was near cracking up. The thought of what he must have sounded like shamed him so he damn near puked. "Look, sir," he said. "What are you holding us for, anyway? You want us to tell you we did something we didn't, but I don't know what it is. And then knocking hell out of us like that . . ."

"You resisted arrest."

"Not in here we didn't resist arrest. How come these guys been batting us around like that? You must be a bunch of sadists, all of you. What if one of us dies, or something?"

"I don't know what you're talking about," said the detective. He asked the cop at the door, "You see anyone get hit around here?"

"No. He's crazy," he answered.

"See?" The detective thought he was a real actor. "Now, look. You tell me what you were doing, and I'll see that you get a break."

"Nothing, I told you."

"All right, then, don't tell me about tonight. But how about on other nights? What have you guys been up to? A little stealing, maybe? Where do you get your marihuana? You been maybe jumping a nice little gringa out in Willow Glen? We haven't got the bastard that pulled that one yet!" He stopped, because his anger was becoming obvious in spite of himself. He said casually, "You know about that, don't you?"

"No."

"Well, then, you heard about it."

"No. I haven't."

"You read the papers, no?"

"Only the sports page—the rest of it's a lot of bull and I don't have time for it."

He did not believe him. "You can't tell me that," he said. "You must read the papers sometimes."

"Sure, sometimes I'll glance at the first page, but I don't even do that very much. I just take the second section and read the sports. Maybe when this happened that you're talking about, I didn't look at the front page."

"Hell, no wonder you people are almost illiterate. How you going to know how to vote when you get old enough?"

"I don't want to vote. I just want to get out of here." He was beginning to feel sick, really sick, and his kidneys hurt him so that he was sure he would be passing blood for a week.

160

"You have to want to vote—it's one right you're guaranteed." He seemed to be a little sorry about that.

"If that's so," said Richard, "then it's my right to not vote if I don't want to vote, isn't it?"

The man dropped it. "This little girl I was telling you about . . . she was walking home from the movies, and three Mexicans pulled her behind a hedge and had some fun."

He seemed to want to keep talking, so Richard asked, "How do you know they were Mexicans?"

"She saw them."

"Yeah, but did she see their birth certificates? Maybe they were Americans?"

The detective looked at him for such a long time that he thought, Oh-oh, I did it this time, but the man had decided a while ago not to use force again. "You're a wise little bastard," he finally said. "Talk pretty good English, too, not like most 'chucos." Again he tried hard not to show his anger, but his voice was loud once more. "You know what I mean when I say Mexican, so don't get so Goddamn smart. She said they were Mexican, that's how we know. Maybe it was your gang."

Richard felt good, because he was certain the detective was going to have to let them go, so he really began to act smart. "We're not a gang," he said. "That is, not a gang the way you mean, only a gang like kids' gangs are, because we grew up together and we played cops-and-robbers, you know. And funny how we used to fight because we all wanted to be the good guys, but now I don't think it was such a good idea, because I just got a pretty good look at the good guys." That jolted the detective a little, and he looked almost embarrassed.

"We have a job to do," he said, explaining everything. "Now, you're sure you guys didn't have anything to do with that?" He said it real cutelike, a sneak punch, and for a moment Richard thought that he would ask where he had been on such-and-such a night, but the detective just smiled his friendly smile.

"I'm sure," Richard said, and smiled right back at him, and one side of his face was so numb that he knew it was

161

not smiling like the other side. "I'm the only Mexican—like *you* say Mexican—in the bunch," he said. "And the others are Spanish, and one is Italian. Besides, I don't know any 'chucos well enough to run around with them."

"Let me see your hands." He looked and was satisfied. "No tattoos. But that's a bad-looking wart you got there."

"I've been playing with frogs," he said sarcastically, but the detective appeared to miss it.

"Better have it taken care of," he said with honest concern. "You still say you don't come from down south?"

"Call up the Santa Clara police, and they'll tell you about me. About all of us."

He was sent into the other room then, and after a while an officer returned their wallets and things and told them they could go. The detective stopped Richard at the door and said:

"So you're going to be a college boy?"

"I guess so." So he *had* checked up.

"Drop in and see me sometime. We can use someone like you when you get older. There are a lot of your people around now, and someone like you would be good to have on the side of law and order."

Jesus Christ! Another one, thought Richard. Aloud he said, "No, thanks. I don't want to have anything to do with you guys."

"Think about it. You have a few years yet. There's a lot you can do for your people that way."

His sincerity surprised Richard. He seemed to mean it. "No," he answered. "I'm no Jesus Christ. Let 'my people' take care of themselves."

"You were defending them a while ago."

"I was defending myself!" *Stupid!*

But who the hell were his people? He had always felt that all people were his people—not in that nauseating God-made-us-all-equal way, for to him that was a deception; the exact opposite was so obvious. But this man, in his attitude and behavior, gave him a new point of view about his world.

Painfully, they walked across town to Ricky's car and somehow made it home. He could not sleep. Things were

162

going on around him that he did not know about. He was amazed at his naïveté. Hearing about Mexican kids being picked up by the police for having done something had never affected him in any way before. Even policemen had never been set aside in his mind as a group. In Santa Clara, where he knew the town marshal and his patrolmen, and always called them by their first names, he did not think of them as cops but as people—in fact, neighbors. One evening had changed all that for him, and now he knew that he would never forget what had happened tonight, and the impression would make him distrust and, in fact, almost hate policemen all his life. Now, for the first time in his life, he felt discriminated against. The horrible thing that he had experienced suddenly was clear, and he cried silently in his bed.

In México they hang the Spaniard, he thought, and here they would do the same to the Mexican, and it was the same person, somehow, doing all this, in another body—in another place. What do they do, these people? That detective, when he is not slapping a face or cajoling or entreating for a confession of some unsolved crime—what does he do when he is not doing this horrible thing he calls a job? Does he have a home, a hearth? A wife upon whom he lavishes all the tenderness in him, whom he holds naked—the only way—to his own nakedness, and in his nakedness is he then real? Or perhaps even—Jesus Christ, NO! NOT CHILDREN! A man like that have children! The wonder of that!

And the guys—they had not said anything, but the way they had looked at him for having stayed in the office so long with that man. "Man," that is truly the worst thing he could possibly call him at this moment. They had been afraid that he had betrayed their trust. Once, on the silent ride home, he had almost exclaimed, "Look, you bastards, I didn't cop out on you. He tried to con me and I conned *him,* and he had to let us go." But he was hurt and a little resentful, and decided they were not worth it. And now they were thinking that if he had not been there, they would not have been accused by association, and therefore not beaten. They were right, of course. And, in a way he

163

had betrayed them, but they did not know this. He had kept his mouth shut, not because of the code but because by co-operating with the police he would have implicated himself. But the guys' loyalty to an unwritten law transcended the fact that they had been at the point of committing a criminal offense, and so much so that they actually forgot this fact. And he knew that from this moment things would not be the same for them again. Something had happened to their relationship, particularly to his relationship with Ricky. More than ever he knew they could never be friends again, because somehow he represented an obstacle to the attainment of certain goals Ricky had imposed upon his life.

He stopped crying then, because it was not worth crying for people. He withdrew into his protective shell of cynicism, but he recognized it for what it was and could easily hide it from the world.

TEN

"This is my brother's daughter from Cholula, don Juan," said Cirilo as Juan Rubio and his son Richard entered his house.

"Much pleasure in knowing you," said Juan Rubio, taking her hand. "Juan Rubio at your command."

"Equally," replied the young girl. "Pilar Ramírez, to serve you."

She turned to Richard, and they exchanged the introduction in the same manner. She was not shy, but appeared so because she was a woman from México. Not since he was a child and his family followed the crops had he seen a woman act like she acted. He was seeing his mother as she had been long ago. She spoke only if directly addressed, and he talked to her. She was from Cholula, in the state of México, she said, and her father was dead and so she was here. He said he had never known anyone from that far south, and she said she was sixteen years old. Once, she giggled as he spoke and he flushed, for he knew she was laughing at his Spanish, which was a California-MexicanAmerican Castilian.

"I am a Pocho," he said, "and we speak like this because here in California we make Castilian words out of English words. But I can read and write in the Spanish, and I taught myself from the time I had but eight years."

"It matters not," she said. "I understand you perfectly well."

She was slight, yet breasty, with good legs, and very dark. And he thought her pretty, because to a Mexican swarthiness means beauty.

The others talked among themselves, so Richard and Pilar were allowed to enjoy their conversation until it was time to leave. He would come back, he thought, for she was interesting and pleasant, and he liked her. She could tell him about the México of today, not that of twenty years ago, which his parents knew.

He never saw her again, but his father did, and occasionally brought back word that she had asked for him, and, in fact, he kidded him about his "admirer." It did not occur to Richard that his father had his eye on her.

Then, one early morning, Richard came home from being with Zelda, to find his house ablaze with lights and his father in a rage. He had never seen him so angry. His face was livid, and when he spoke, saliva sprayed with his words and some trickled down the corner of his mouth.

"My daughters will not behave like whores!" he shouted.

"If I am a whore, it is having your blood that makes me one!" Luz stood up to him, shouting back.

"What hour is this—three o'clock in the morning—for a decent girl to be coming home?" he asked. "Where were you?"

"That is no concern of yours," she replied. "What I do is my business!"

The children were huddled against a wall, the smaller ones crying. Consuelo, in a soiled robe, also shrank back, she alone knowing what wrath could drive her husband to do.

"Tell me where you were!" he insisted. "This is still my house, and as long as you are in it, you answer to me!"

"Wake up!" screamed Luz, and her face was ugly. "This *your* house!" She laughed shrilly. "This is our house, and if we want, we can have you put out! Tell him, Mamá. He put the house in your name, in case something happened to him you would have no trouble! *Tell him, Mamá!*" she screamed. "Tell him something has happened to him!"

Juan Rubio hit her with the back of his hand, and she bounced off the wall but she did not fall. Again she screamed to Consuelo, and Consuelo, given courage by the utterance of that which she had lately been telling her daughters, lost her head and stepped forward, screeching, "Do not dare to touch her again, you brute!" She took hold of his arm, and he spun toward her, the force of his movement knocking her off balance, so she stumbled crazily through the door and landed on her face in the kitchen.

Richard stood on the opposite side, transfixed by the grotesque masque that was taking place before his eyes. A masque it surely was, for he did not know any of these people. In his mind, he was not sure any of it was real. Horrified and in anguish, he thought, *A bad dream! A real bad dream or a Goddamn dumb show!*

His sister brought him out of shock. "Stand there! Just stand there, you weak bastard, and watch this son of a bitch hit your mother!" She leaped at Juan Rubio's face with her hands, and very deliberately he hit her in the face with his fist. She did not get up.

Juan Rubio rushed out the door and down into the cellar. From his tool closet he took an axe, and began first on the wine barrels and then on the shelves upon shelves of preserves, and when he was done destroying everything he had built or accumulated with his own hands, he walked into the house, a specter drenched in wine, purple and ominous. "Out!" he shouted. "Out, everyone, for I am going to destroy this cancer!" But his family was incapable of moving, their fear was so great, and as he walked toward the cupboard, Richard tackled him from behind. Crying, tears streaming down his face, he pleaded, "No, Papá! No, Papá! It is worth nothing—all this!" And all the time he held on to the kicking legs of his father, and when he was shaken off and they were both on their feet, his father hit him a chopping blow with his great hand, and once more turned to what was now a duty. Richard came back again, dripping blood from his nose and mouth, and this time he jumped on his father's back, only to slip off, and as he fell his head struck the floor, knocking him unconscious.

Juan Rubio laid the axe almost gently on the table and picked up his son as easily as he would a child. He carried him into the bedroom and put him on the bed.

"Get water!" he said to his wife, who was tearing at her hair, screaming, "My son! My son!" But at that moment Richard opened his eyes.

He saw that the walls of the room were still standing and that his father and mother were there over him, strangely close together. His upper lip was numb, and he could feel a swelling along his nostrils. He tried to get up, but his father held him down.

"Get me a change of clothes," said Juan Rubio. "And make me a mochila of some of my things."

"Bueno, Juan," she said simply.

"You are leaving, then, my father?" asked Richard.

"Yes, but do not be disturbed. I will remain in the valley."

"It is time," said Richard, "and I am not disturbed. I am sad, true, but I am somehow happy."

Juan Rubio did not look at his son. Perhaps it was because of the many things that would remain unsaid between them. Finally, he looked into his son's eyes. "Yes," he said. "It is time, and I have waited overly long, but

167

since I am able to do it after all, it was not wrong to wait. Do not cry, my son." He wiped a tear from Richard's face with the side of his thumb.

Richard took the hand that had always been at once so tender and so harsh. "I cannot keep myself from crying. Rare that always in this family I remember tears. When we are happy we cry, and when we have tragedy we cry."

Juan Rubio smiled. "That is because in the end we are Mexican. It is as simple as that," he said. "Once, I had an acquaintance"—and he laughed now as he spoke, so that his beautiful unbrushed teeth shone yellow—"who said that Mexicans were the most fortunate people in the world, because they ate strong chile and cried. When a Mexican has stomach trouble, this man said, it is usually a serious illness and he dies, but he will never have boils in the intestines or any of that sort of trouble. That is because we eat chile and are a lachrymose race."

"You did not like him, did you?"

"Why do you ask that?"

"Because you called him your acquaintance and 'this man.'"

"Well, he was not an intimate friend. We came to California together. He was a strange one; in fact I thought at times that he was one of 'those others.'"

"They have their place," said Richard.

Juan Rubio again looked into his son's eyes. "You have that much understanding, my son? . . . Then I think I can tell you that for a long time I thought you would become like that. Because you had the bad lot to live with a houseful of girls, and your mother protected you so much. I thought that if it happened so, I would try to understand it. And yet—I suppose because you are the only man in the family—I thought I would strangle you with my own hands, and to do that would mean that I would destroy myself, because although I have never told you, I feel about you as strongly as your mother does."

"I know."

Juan Rubio was not embarrassed. It seemed that he had all the time in the world to talk to his son, and what had happened a few minutes ago seemed forgot. "This acquaintance I spoke about, he is a writer."

"That is what I will be," said Richard.

"Do you want that more than anything?"

"Yes, my father. More than anything, and forgive me if I put that before you and my mother."

"There is nothing to forgive," said Juan Rubio. "Only, never let anything stand in your way of it, be it women, money, or—what people talk about today—position. Only that, promise me—that you will be true unto yourself, unto what you honestly believe is right. And, if it does not stand in your way, do not ever forget that you are Mexican." It was Juan Rubio who was now crying.

"I could never forget that!" said Richard.

"One more thing," said his father. "I did not purposely strike your mother. I could not do that to you. Willingly I would tear this heart out with my hands when I hurt you in that way."

"I know."

"I go now," said Juan Rubio. "The sun will soon come out."

"You will be all right now, Papá?"

"I am all right *now*. I feel I am a man again."

"That is good," said Richard. Juan Rubio reached the door, and Richard said, "Papá."

He turned, and his son said, "¿Un abrazo?" They put their arms around each other in the Mexican way. Then Juan Rubio kissed his son on the mouth.

In the other room, Luz finally picked herself up off the floor and disappeared into her room.

On the bed, Richard heard the sound of the automobile fade away. Forgive me, my father, he thought. Forgive me because I cannot really talk with you, and for my transgressions against you. And I am sorry your life is very nearly spent. Soon, he knew, his father would be with another woman, for it was impossible that he should live without one. And he was happy for that, but, in spite of his intelligence, he was deeply hurt that he should have a woman other than his mother. He could never understand that part of himself—how he could feel in two distinct ways about something, with each feeling equally strong. This was one of the things he could not discuss with his father.

The tears were drying on his cheeks when he walked out of the room. His mother's face was flushed. He could see the regret and sorrow she would not admit even to herself. She moved about in a glow of victory, puttered here and there doing nothing whatsoever, but seemingly busy. Then she began to sweep the house, and the symbolism was so starkly real to him at that moment that he ran out the rear door, and, clutching at the trunk of the walnut tree, he uttered painful sobs until there were no tears left. After a bit, he went back into the kitchen and got a plateful of beans and some cold tortillas. He sat down to eat, and his mother said:

"I could have got that for you." She was suddenly full of solicitude, conscientious in her duty to the man of the house. Everything seemed to remind him. Things went badly for him, but he knew he must survive the next hour or he could never live with his mother again. The food was tasteless, even when smothered with chile. She tried to take his plate from in front of him. "Your food is cold. Let me warm it for you," she said.

"It is worth nothing, Mamá," he said. "Let it remain as it is." He could not tell her that it was impossible for him to have her do anything for him at this time.

She sat across from him and began to cry. "I cannot endure the knowledge that you are eating cold food," she said. "That is the reason I am here—your mother—to see that you are taken care of. Time enough when you are married to have to cook for yourself, and wash and iron for yourself and your wife, here in this country where all wives are lazies."

It was difficult to be cruel to her, particularly at this time, but he must do something that might stop the torture of continuing this conversation. In her ignorance, she was tearing him up inside. "Like my father had to do for himself, Mamá?" he asked.

"You are on his side," she sobbed. "If so, why did you not go with him?" With her it was still a matter of sides, and he tried to explain how he felt. And now he was pitying her.

"Mamá," he said, "there is no such thing in my mind. I have not gone with my father because you need me more—that is why. I love you both, but I do not love one of you more than the other, and if it fell upon his lot to need me, then I would go to him. You yourself, I know, would be unhappy if I forsook him. But what is between the two of you is not my affair. I am not provoked that he left. I am sorry that it had to be so, but I am not provoked, and I do not wish even to discuss whatever has happened between you. The only thing for me in the matter is that you are my mother and he is my father. Nothing else is changed. I am not changed, and I can never be changed by that which is outside of me. I can only be loyal to you both as well as I can."

She stopped crying. "You are right in many ways, my son. But he has deserted his wife and children. . . ."

"I will not discuss it, Mamá. Now or ever."

She did not mention his father again, but she began to talk of the new life they must make without him, and she sounded almost happy. Now that she was certain Richard would remain with her, she did not have the need to arouse his sympathy. He realized how frightened she had been. "You are the head of the family now, Richard. You are the man of the house," she said. "I know how much you wanted to go to the university, and I am filled with sadness that you will not be able to do so, for it is your duty to take care of us." It did not matter to him that she was sincere in her concern about that, and that she had somehow completely absolved herself of any taint of guilt for what had happened. But he could not allow her to believe that he was doing this for any reason other than the fact that he desired to do it.

"It is not a duty, Mamá," he said. "I am doing what I am doing because I do not want to do anything else at the moment, but please do not mistake my motives. It would

171

only make you hurt much later. I told you it is not my life which has been changed, but yours and my father's. I do not belong here any more. I do not even belong in this town any more, and when the time comes that I want to go to school, Mamá, I will do so. I will remain until I must leave, and that is all."

She smiled, and through her smile he knew that she did not believe him. She was so full of plans now that she was like a child, so he reached across and kissed her cheek. "We should all go together to the church, little son," she said. "We are now starting on a new life, and it would be a good thing to receive a blessing from the Lord." It was suddenly too much once more, and now he must really hurt her.

"You received one blessing already when you were married, full of sacredness and solemnity. It did not help. No, Mamá. You go to your church and light the candles to your God. I am finished with such things."

Her face was white, and for a moment he thought that she would fall from her chair. "What are you saying? What blasphemy is this?"

He said, "Please, Mamá. I do not wish to make you unhappy, but you are forcing me to do so. I have left the Church. It is now a long time that I have not been to Mass, although I have believed all along. But now I find that I am through believing. I have not told you of this, because of what it would do to you—of what it is doing to you."

"You do not believe! What is this you do not believe? You do not believe what?"

"I no longer believe in God," he said, and was surprised at himself that he had dared finally to say the thing aloud. The maybe-maybe-what-if-I'm-wrong? thoughts did not come to his mind, and the apprehension and dizzy feeling that he always experienced at such thoughts did not come, and at last he was really free.

She cried then, long, painful sobs, and he did nothing to comfort her, for he was out of it completely. When she calmed down a bit, she questioned, striving to find an explanation for this tragedy. She was not angry—she could not even feel sorry for him yet, her torment was so great.

His life! How could he possibly live the good life? Without Christian principles, his children would suffer, and, worse, he could never teach them goodness without the help of the true faith. She found many such arguments to negate the words he had just spoken, but in the end it was simply "Why? WHY?"

In spite of himself, he could not remain indifferent to her. He went to his knees beside her and held her close. "It is a very difficult thing, my mother, to make you understand. It was most difficult for me to arrive at my final conclusion about religion. Now it is impossible for me to continue living a lie. I am good, though. Even in the way that you mean 'good' I am good, and in my way I am a better Christian than most Christians I know. And if my behavior can be called Christian, it is because I agree with most of the Decalogue and not because it is a Christian thing to do so. I do not like some of the things they do, these Christians. I do not have to fear God in order to love man. That is one of my weaknesses, perhaps—that I love man too much. Nor do I need God in my hour of strongest need.

"But you, Mamá, you must believe, because for you it is not a lie—because you could not live without your God. Without Him, you would be dead before you really die."

She accepted her defeat, and it was clear to him that as long as she could keep him by her side, nothing else mattered. Her love for him was so strong that even his renunciation of the eternal life was not too great for her to suffer. It was not too healthy, this thing, she knew. Yet it was bearable, because she realized that she had but a small part of him. She had lost her men—both of them. And already there was a look of mourning on her face— An emblem more convincing than if she had donned black garments.

Outside, light grayness replaced the dark, and Richard was happy the night was over, for, indeed, bad things happened at night.

173

ELEVEN

That summer, Richard and Ricky graduated from high school, and after the summer fruit work was terminated, they went to work in a steel mill. Soon they were earning so much money that their friends also quit school and took jobs. On Richard's instigation, early in the summer they had all gone to the parish priest, and for the small fee of two dollars apiece the priest had given them affidavits that made them old enough to work. The fellows had not wanted to do it, because they thought Father Moore would be angry with them, but Richard insisted, and they went and he talked. Father Moore made fourteen dollars.

After a few weeks in the role of breadwinner, Richard sensed that a sense of duty was taking a strong hold on him. Since his father was no longer at home, full responsibility for the discipline of the family, as well as for its maintenance, had slowly been pushed upon him by his mother, and in spite of his resentment at her for taking such unfair advantage of him, and an occasional twinge of pain he felt when he realized that he was taking the place that rightfully belonged to his father, he knew that actually it was the only thing to be done in order that the family should survive.

As long as I am here, he told himself, this thing I must do. Until I go away—until then only.

But slowly the temporary aspect of the situation was giving way to permanency, and he was frightened because the whole thing was getting out of hand, and he himself was more and more responsible for it. He was aware that his mother knew. Give him some responsibility—he could almost invade her thoughts—and he will see for himself what his life should now be. And he knew he could still say, I don't give a Goddamn about any of them—let them take care of themselves! But by now it was not true even if he could verbalize such thoughts. It would be a different thing, his leaving them. If the deed was to be done, in fact, he must leave in spite of his concern and love for them—in spite of his now strong belief that he should remain. The desire to go away must of necessity be stronger. And his emancipation would be all the more dear for it, he thought. But, too—how true—it would also be so much more difficult to attain; perhaps it was an impossibility.

Thus, as the days became weeks and then months, life went on for Richard Rubio. He worked, ate, and slept; he did very little else. On Saturday mornings, the boys played football or drove into the City to watch a football game. An occasional movie or a dance—always in a group with the guys, except for the times when he saw Zelda, and that was not too often these days. Then, one day, he thought, What the hell am I doing? And he began once again to spend some time in the library, and enrolled in a course in Creative Writing at night school.

He did not learn a thing about writing, but was thrown into contact with people with whom he could talk. His new friends were older and thought him a very interesting subject, and he was happy listening to them, because they were educated and liberals and introduced him to new adventures in reading. But then he began to understand them and did not agree with some of their ideas, because they constituted a threat to his individuality, and his individuality was already in jeopardy. And it bothered him that they should always try to find things in his life that could make him a martyr of some sort, and it pained him when they insisted he dedicate his life to the Mexican cause, because it was the same old story, and he was quite sure he did not really believe there was a Mexican cause—at least not in the world with which he was familiar. They thought him very interesting some more, and showed him off, but they made the mistake of thinking him a child, and in the end it turned out badly, because one of them, a Marxist, became very middle-class when he found Richard in bed with his extremely pretty wife. They dropped him then, for she was not the only one.

The gang was together one evening, having a beer at the poolhall, killing time until they should decide what to do with the evening. Suddenly Ricky said:

"What the hell's the matter with you, anyway, Richard? You don't wanta be around us guys any more?"

"What are you talking about?" he answered.

"You always been a funny bastard," Ricky continued, "but now you got those highfalutin friends, and you been getting the big head or something—too Goddamn good for your old buddies."

Richard smiled that Ricky should feel this way and admit it. "Nothing wrong with me," he said. "I just have a lot on my mind these days."

"Boy, you must," said Ricky. "You really must. If I didn't work with you, I probably wouldn't get to see you at all. Even at work, you never want to talk to a guy any more."

"Oh, why the hell don't you lay off 'im, Ricky?" said one of the other boys. "You're beginning to sound like an old snatch."

Richard looked at the other boy with new respect. Hell, he had known him all his life, and he had always thought of him as a dumb kid. The boy was always so in awe of Ricky, and now he was passing him in understanding.

Ricky was angry and showed it. "Hell, this guy's getting too smart for everybody now. I was talking to his old lady, and she says he don't even go to church any more, and she can't even talk to him like his mother any more, 'cause he don't want her advice on anything." He looked at Richard and became friendly so suddenly that Richard knew he was sincerely concerned about him. "You're our buddy, Richard. You been our buddy all our lives. Hell, we don't want ya to go wrong."

For the first time in his life, Richard knew that Ricky really liked him. Why, he would not even venture to guess.

176

Perhaps even Ricky could not tell him why, but he knew intuitively that Ricky liked him so much that he also hated him.

"What the hell's the matter with you?" asked the other boy again. "So the guy doesn't wanna go to church—who the hell does? Jeez, how many times I been with you and we never even got close to the church and you told your old lady you went to Mass? Why don't you knock it off, for Christ's sake?"

But Richard was interested and still amused, so he asked, "What are you talking about, Rick? What do you mean, 'go wrong'?"

"You know what I mean . . . running around with all kinds of funny people—all those pachucos you got for buddies. Lucky you haven't ended up in juvenile or Preston, or something. And these other guys I seen you with. One time, I saw you in San Jose with a couple of guys that looked queer as hell. Jesus, I know you're okay, but it don't do you no good to be seen with guys like that."

"Oh, hell, Ricky," said Richard. "Now you're talking about yourself, not about me. It don't do *you* no good to be seen with a guy like me who is seen with guys like that. Especially since you're gonna be a big businessman and join the Chamber of Commerce or some Goddamn club they got for guys like you." Then he stopped and changed his voice, because he could not hurt Ricky like this. "There's really nothing wrong with knowing all kinds of people. Those pachuc's you were talking about are real nice guys, and if they ever do anything wrong—well, that's their business; I don't have to take a part in it. If I know a guy who stole something, that doesn't make me a crook, does it? And those two guys you were talking about—they're queer, and they have a bunch of friends that are the same way, but they're real intelligent and good people. They just happen to be like that, that's all. Like a guy with only one leg, or a deaf-and-dumb guy, or a guy with the con. They can't help it, but they make the most of their life. And, another thing—they like being that way, and they never fool with me, because they know I'm straight, and I respect them for that. Those two guys live together, and

177

they really love each other. You ought to see them, how nice they talk to each other and the way they take care of one another. Hell, even married people don't act that good."

Ricky thought for a moment, and then said, "I guess you're right, in a way, but, just the same, if they're fruit, they're fruit, and that just isn't right. I'm glad you're not fooling around with those guys any more."

Richard was relieved that Ricky had decided to let his remark about the Chamber of Commerce pass. He ordered another beer, and the old Spaniard who owned the pool-hall brought it to him surreptitiously, because he knew they were under age. "Come on, you guys, think of something to do, for Christ's sake! Goddamn, this town is dead!" exclaimed Ricky, and Richard thought, Saturday night is the only time worth living for some people—a lot of people live just for Saturday night. What a Goddamn existence! And Thomas Nakano said, "Let's go to Watsonville," and Richard thought, Christ! And everybody laughed because they had forgotten Thomas was even there.

But Ricky said, "Yeah. That's the best thing anybody said tonight. Let's go to Watsonville, you guys."

"What the hell for?" said Richard, meaning it was not worth the long ride, but Thomas misunderstood him and said:

"Get our nuts out of hock!"

Everyone but Richard agreed. He thought of the time he and Ricky were present when the big guys in the neighborhood were going to a hookshop, and was suddenly depressed because he was in the pattern and they now, here in the poolroom, must look as ridiculous as the big guys of long ago had. Now he was one of the big guys, and he saw clearly that if he allowed himself to be carried along in the stream of life in Santa Clara, he would one day soon be one of the older guys, and then, finally, one day he would be just another old fart around town, bullshitting on a streetcorner with another old fart—Ricky, probably—about how it used to be in the old days. "Naw," he said, "I'm getting mine. All you guys who aren't making out, go ahead." And no one said, "Why don'tcha fix us all up

178

with Zelda?" Because they all thought she was still his girl, just as she did. Instead, Ricky said:

"Aw, come on. It's no fun going up there unless all the gang goes. Like old times."

Jesus! Did he have to say that? "I can't see paying two bucks for a couple of minutes of fun," said Richard. "And now it probably costs five, what with all the horny soldiers up at Ord."

"We'll chip in and pay for you," said Ricky. "Hell, we know how rough it is with you, now your old man's took off."

"Okay. What's the difference?" said Richard. "But you have to let me drive and we take a bottle, 'cause I can't see going all the way out there for just the ride—I'm not going to get laid. And we have to get back early. You guys'd think nothing of riding around all night."

Ricky was too happy with the thought that they were not going to waste the Saturday night, after all, to make a remark about the demands Richard was imposing. "Hell, we'll get back early," he said. "I gotta get back early anyway, 'cause I promised my girl I'd take her to six-thirty Mass tomorrow morning."

Richard shook his head in amazement at Ricky's complete lack of sense and made the sign of the cross. He drove the car as fast as it would go. They went through Morgan Hill at ninety-five miles an hour, and suddenly he had the thought that he was trying to commit suicide, and stopped the car. The guys laughed, because they could see that he was shaking, and thought he had frightened himself before he could frighten them.

Just what the hell is it I want to do? he thought.

In the bright sunlight of a Santa Clara Christmas, he thought of past Christmases, and those days, which had not been especially tender ones at the time, now in the gilt of retrospect seemed warm and wonderful. And now the war. He had a strong, almost overpowering desire to win the war singlehandedly. He did not believe in killing, and what in spite of that conviction would have been romantic of itself at one time was not romantic now.

But he sought glory because he was now a part of the infinite nonentity—the worker, the family man. He had slowly dropped into oblivion even in his mind, the one place where once he had soared above the multitude.

What to do? What to do? Even death I can think of, he thought. But, no, not death—the finality of it. Silly. That old fear still haunts me. . . . If I could be dead like the man on the flying trapeze . . . it would be not only welcome but a privilege to be dead that way—perfect in unaliveness —released from the hell of being alive, from making decisions that will only serve to make living more of a hell. . . . Nirvana, or whatever the hell the Hindus call it . . . that way, yes—conditioned for that, I would be dead, but not in the way I know of death. Yet, though I know it and think of it as the only panacea, I fear to be unalive.

And then January, and what he must do he must do soon or forever hold his peace. They played football on the primaryschool field. Touchtackle was not exciting enough now, for the war was a few weeks old; and so by unspoken agreement they played tackle on the hard ground. It did not matter that they were in street clothes, and the bruises and skinned knees were a welcome thing— almost a pleasure. Driven by an almost masochistic impulse, they did little talking or shouting, as youngsters will do in the spirit of play; rather, they played harder and harder, not knowing why they were doing it. There was nothing important for them these days except the thought that soon they would be old enough to enlist, or, in the event their parents did not consent, they would soon be drafted.

They stopped their game and sat around talking about enlisting together. Richard never spoke about it the way they did, because he did not know what he was to do about the war. Now, this day, he noticed that Ricky was not so enthusiastic as the others. Finally the others noticed it, and everyone became quiet, looking at Ricky until his face got red and he began to talk in an excited voice.

"Look, you guys, I know you're not going to like it, but I hafta look out for myself, and I'm not going with you, because I'm going to Officer Candidate School!" They

180

were silent, and he blurted out, "Well, I hafta look out for myself, you guys! And I get sent to Notre Dame or maybe U.S.C. or something, so I already signed up to take the tests, and old Dingleberries at the high school is going to help me study for it, even though I graduated already."

They were all too amazed to talk about it. And they were hurt also, but such a betrayal by Ricky was not entirely unexpected. An officer! And all their older brothers ever wrote home about the service was what big pricks officers were, and now their buddy was going to be an officer!

Richard felt envy such as he had never felt before. Not because Ricky was going to be an officer, but because he was going to go to college. "You'll make it, too, Ricky," he said, and he knew that Ricky was right. He had to look out for himself, and he would make Goddamn sure he made it. It was so like him to have a despised teacher tutor him for the examinations, because Ricky was smart enough to know that Dingleberries was a good teacher, no matter how much he hated him. "And if any of these guys end up under your command, for Christ's sake treat 'em nice," he added. His words sounded a little phony and they did not ease the tension, but he was happy that the constriction in his chest had disappeared.

Ricky smiled and said, "I been thinking about it, Richard. Why don't you go with me? We can still take the exams at the same time, and old Dingleberries'll help you if I ask him to."

"No, Rick. I'm sorry as hell I can't do it. I probably won't be joining anything. I won't get in unless I get drafted, and there's not much chance of that, because I'm too young, and then I got so many dependents."

They had been so engrossed that they did not notice that Thomas Nakano had joined them until he spoke. "I just come to say goodbye, you guys," he said. The boys looked at him shamefacedly. Since the war had begun, they had avoided him tactlessly. He knew their discomfiture, and it embarrassed him. "I got nothing to do with the war, fellas," he said. "I'm an American, just like you guys. I just come to say goodbye, 'cause we gotta go away

181

to a relocation center in a few days, an' I don't know if I'll get to see you guys before I leave."

They all said goodbye, and somehow the fact that Thomas was to be removed from their lives made it easier to be friends with him again for a few minutes. Richard was sorry for all of them. "How about the ranch, Thomas?" he asked. "What's your old man going to do with the ranch?"

Thomas seemed unconcerned, but his voice broke as he spoke. "After this week, we ain't gonna have no more ranch. My old man says we can't pay off the mortgage if we can't harvest the crop, so the bank is gonna foreclose," he said. He was thoughtful for a moment. "You know," he continued, in command of his voice again, "my old man's been on that land since before the last war, too. And my mother's been helping work the Goddamn ground since she was fourteen, when my old man and her was married. Alla us was born there, for Christ's sake. She never went to no hospital." He began to cry. It was bad watching Thomas cry, but after a while he said, "I got nothing to do with this Goddamn war, but Jesus I wish I could join up with you guys. I'd kill a shitpot full of the bastards for screwing up my life!" The boys did not know what to say to him, and suddenly it was not necessary to say anything, because he became the old Thomas once again. "You know," he said, and his eyes disappeared in his grin, "they told my old man they're sending us to Santa Anita at first—you know, to the race track. Then from there they'll send us to Wyoming or Utah or some Goddamn place like that. Gonna be colder'n hell, too, I bet. Anyway, I'm gonna try to get Seabiscuit's stall if I can, so's I can be a kinda celebrity. An' you know what else I been thinking? Well, they're putting all the Japanese people in these camps, and everybody'll be Jap, and I won't know how to act around a nisei girl. Funny how I never got into a nisei in my life; anyway, I'll find out if it's true or not."

The boys were laughing naturally when he finished, and they began to punch him around, and called him a crazy bastard. They ended up wrestling on the ground, so

182

that by the time Thomas had to leave, he was able to leave as one of the gang.

"I wanna say goodbye to your mother, okay, Richard?" asked Thomas.

"Hell, yes!" They walked away together. When they were alone, Thomas said:

"In a way I'm glad we're going away, 'cause things are getting kinda rough for Japanese people around here."

"You have to expect people to feel funny, Thomas. But it's like you said—they have nothing to do with what happened, either. All we ever get to know about wars is that we have to fight them. People are funny about things anyway, without wars to make them funnier."

"Yeah," said Thomas, "but things are happening."

Richard knew what Thomas meant, but still he tried to show how things come to pass. "You mean that guy that was killed in Morgan Hill? Well, in the first place, I don't even know whether it's really true, and, in the second place, if it is true, the guys who are supposed to have done it are Filipinos, and, hell, those guys are right off the boat, and I guess they really think they're getting back at Japan that way. And then the family that had their house burned —well, they got the guys that did it, and they'll probably let them go, I know, but they're almost from overseas, too, 'cause they're from the South and you know how they are —anyone who isn't a white man *gotta be showed his place like we do 'em back home!*"

Thomas did not speak, and Richard thought he had hurt his friend's feelings. "Look, Thomas, you know I don't feel that way, don't you?"

"I know that, Richard. You're the only one a the guys who hasn't made me feel like I bombed Pearl Harbor. It's just that something happened to me the other night, and I can't feel too good about how people are acting."

"What?"

"I went to see my girl—my ex, I mean, 'cause she don't like me no more now, on account of the war. She been sneaking out to talk to me, now and then, but that night she told me no more . . . and then these guys jumped me and kicked the piss out of me. I didn't even get to hit even one of them at least, 'cause I wasn't expecting them to beat me up, being I knew them from school and a couple of guys from my old scout troop. They hurt my feelings more than anything else, but they give me a good going over."

"Who were they?" asked Richard.

"Oh, you know—that whole DeMolay outfit."

"Jesus Christ!" Richard exclaimed in disgust. This was it! Now he was getting out! *If you ever need a favor,* the Rooster had said.

The Rooster had told him that it would take a day or two to get the gang together. "We have to do it as soon as possible," he said, "because I'm going into the Marines in a few days, and the rest of the guys are joining up, too."

"Let me know as soon as you're ready," said Richard. "This is something that has to be taken care of."

"I been thinking," said the Rooster. "You know these guys pretty good, huh?"

"Yeah."

"Then you better just take me around there to show me where they hang out, and then don't come around at all, because you'll be in bad trouble if they recognize you."

It had not been in his mind to do anything like that, and he told the Rooster so, but in the end the boy was right and they planned it that way.

"I'll call you and let you know when it happens," said the Rooster.

He waited for the telephone call, and finally on the fourth day it came. "It's been taken care of," he said.

"Thanks, man."

"I'll see you after the war, Richard. I'll be leaving in the morning."

That was all. He had not wanted to give him any of the details. In the morning, the newspaper carried the story on the first page. An unprovoked attack by pachucos upon a group of boys had put two youths in the hospital with broken limbs.

It was bad, thought Richard. It was all wrong. What he had done was as wrong as what they had done to Thomas. It had been like a small battle in the big war, and

184

that war was also wrong. Even to take a small part in it was wrong, but now he must also go to war. It was his only alternative—to get away from this place was the only good he could get from it.

His mother and sisters were quietly serious at lunchtime. Engrossed in his own thoughts, he did not notice it until his mother said, "Your father came today. He wants me to divorce him."

He wondered why this information should affect him so. His father was gone and would never come back; he knew that. And yet the finality, the irrevocability, that such a thing as divorce implied shook him so much that he realized he had never believed it to be completely over for his parents. When he did not speak, she said:

"He is living with a woman, and apparently he wants to be married to her. An old man like himself, and she is young enough to be your sister."

"Who is she?" he asked.

"I do not know her," said Consuelo. "But a harlot she must be for certain. He said to tell you her name is Pilar."

Pilar! And he suddenly laughed.

"You know her!" his mother accused. "And why do you laugh?"

"Yes, Mamá. You would not understand why I laugh. It is something related to incest." He sobered once more. "But did you not expect a thing like that to happen sometime? Surely you must have known he would not live alone! His house fell down, and he must build himself another one, else die."

"He is living in sin," she said. "And now there is to be a child, and the child will be born of sin, because I am his wife and will remain his wife until I die!" She was in a frenzy of righteous wrath. "That woman dares call herself Rubio—I am the only woman of Rubio in the eyes of God, and they will burn in Hell!"

He could not eat. He sat shuddering in his chair, looking at his mother, and could not believe that she was saying such things. She must be going mad! They say when they approach that time of life it is possible. He thought of this unborn child and was jealous—a boy it would be, because things always happen like that. There was nothing to be done now except run away from the insidious tragedy of such an existence. And it came to him that it was all very wrong, somehow, that he should think of himself at this time. All very wrong that he should use the war, a thing he could not believe in, to serve his personal problem.

He was crying when he started to speak, but by the time he was finished, he was talking in a strong voice. "I am leaving, my mother. I am going into the service today, if they will accept me. At any rate, I go now to enlist. The girls are working now and I will send you money, so that you do not need me here any more."

She did not make the scene he had expected. "I have been teaching myself to expect this, my son," she said. "But you are wrong, and you know it. I need you more than life itself." It did not matter to her that her children were listening. "You are my favorite—my only one, truly. For you I would trade them all; every one of them I would send off to the war if I could keep you here with me."

I should really hate her, he thought, but I cannot. He looked at his sisters, and they returned his look quietly, wordlessly. "She doesn't mean it the way it sounds," he said to them, in English. "She's very lonely, and a little heartsick, and her jealousy makes her proud—too proud to admit that she wants Papá back. That is all—try to understand her as long as you remain with her." He changed his speech into Spanish without pause. "I go now, Mamá, to find my father. He will go with me and sign the papers. But I will be here for a week or so, even if I am accepted today. They always give you a week or so."

But in San Francisco that evening Richard Rubio and a hundred other such young men were sworn into the Navy of the United States. He had his dinner on a train en route to the training station. Afterward he lay in an upper berth listening to the chatter of his new companions, thinking little of the life he had left behind—only of the future, and suddenly he was afraid he might be killed. If it came, he would not be ready for it—no, he would never be prepared to die, but he could do nothing about it. He would come back, he thought, making himself believe it for a moment.

He thought of all the beautiful people he had known. Of his father and mother in another time; of Joe Pete Manõel and of Marla Jamison; of Thomas and of Zelda and of Mayrie—the Rooster and Ricky. Yes, even Ricky had been beautiful. What of them—and why? Of what worth was it all? His father had won his battle, and for him life was worth while, but he had never been unaware of what his fight was. *But what about me?* thought Richard. Because he did not know, he would strive to live.

He thought of this and he remembered, and suddenly he knew that for him there would never be a coming back.

José Antonio Villarreal was born and has spent most of his life in California, although he has traveled extensively over the course of the years. The son of a Mexican migrant worker, he received his degree from the University of California at Berkeley in 1950 after four years in the Navy. He has since lived and taught in Mexico, Colorado, California, and Texas. He is also the author of *The Fifth Horseman* and *Clemente Chacón* and is currently working on a sequel to *Pocho*.